DEADLINE DELIVERY

A 'You Say Which Way' Adventure
by
Peter Friend

Big hugs to the Monkey Lab writing group for all their ideas, criticism, picky line editing and baking.

Published by:
The Fairytale Factory Ltd.
Wellington, New Zealand.
All rights reserved.
Copyright Peter Friend © 2015

ISBN-13: 978-1522878476
ISBN-10: 1522878475

How This Book Works

- This story depends on YOU.

- YOU say which way the story goes.

- What will YOU do?

At the end of each chapter, you get to make a decision. Turn to the page that matches your choice – for example, **P62** means turn to page 62.

You're just another poor kid living in the flooded under-city. Life is hard every day, especially for a courier like you, delivering packages to the under-city's most dangerous neighborhoods, while dodging pirate gangs, wild animals and security robots. But today is no normal day – today, you might end up as an explorer, or a froggy, or a trainee manager. Or dead. Or worse. It's your choice. Be careful out there.

Oh … and watch out for crocodiles and the two-legged dog.

Dispatch Office

Out of breath from climbing stairs, you finally reach Level 8 of Ivory Tower. Down the hallway, past a tattoo parlor, Deadline Delivery's neon sign glows red. The word Dead flickers as you approach.

It's two minutes past seven in the morning – is Deadline Delivery's dispatch office open yet? Yes, through the mesh-covered window in the steel door, Miss Betty is slouched behind her cluttered desk. You knock and smile as if you want to be here.

Miss Betty turns and scowls at you. Nothing personal – she scowls at everyone. She presses a button and the steel door squeaks and squeals open.

"Good morning, ma'am. Got any work for me today?" you ask.

She sighs, scratches her left armpit, and taps at her computer. Then she rummages through a long shelf of packages and hands you a plastic-wrapped box and two grimy dollar coins. "Urgent delivery," she says. "Pays ten bucks, plus toll fees."

Ten dollars is more than usual. Suspicious, you check the box's delivery label. "390 Brine Street? That's in the middle of pirate territory!"

She shrugs. "If you're too scared, there are plenty of other kids who'll do it."

Scared? You're terrified. But you both know she's right –

if you don't take this job, someone else will. And you really need the money – you have exactly three dollars in the whole world, and your last meal was lunch yesterday. "Thank you, Miss Betty."

"Uniform," she says, pointing to the box of Deadline Delivery caps.

You pick up the least dirty cap. What's that stink? Has something died in it? You swap it for the second-least dirty one and put that on. You'd rather not wear any kind of uniform – sometimes it's better to not attract attention in public – but Miss Betty insists.

The steel door squeaks and starts to close, and you hurry out. Miss Betty doesn't say goodbye. She never does.

After stashing the package in your backpack and the toll coins in your pocket, you hurry down the stairs to the food court on Level 5. Time to grab a quick breakfast. This might be your last meal ever, and there's no sense in dying hungry. This early in the morning, only Deep-Fried Stuff and Mac's Greasy Spoon are open, so there's not a lot of choice.

In Mac's Greasy Spoon, Mac himself cuts you a nice thick slice of meatloaf for a dollar, and you smile and thank him, even though his meatloaf is always terrible. If there's any meat in it, you don't want to know what kind. At least it's cheap and filling. After a few bites, you wrap the rest in a plastic bag and put it in your pocket for lunch.

You walk back down the stairs to Ivory Tower's main entrance on Level 3. Levels 1 and 2 are somewhere further down, underwater, but you've never seen them. The polar ice caps melted and flooded the city before you were born.

From beside the bulletproof glass doors, a bored-looking guard looks up. "It's been quiet out there so far this morning," she tells you, as she checks a security camera screen. "But there was pirate trouble a few blocks north of the Wall last night. And those wild dogs are roaming around again too. Be careful, kid."

The doors grind open, just a crack, enough for you to squeeze through and out onto Nori Road. Well, everyone calls it a road, although the actual road surface is twenty feet under the murky water. Both sides of the so-called road have sidewalks of rusty girders and planks and bricks and other junk, bolted or welded or nailed to the buildings – none of it's too safe to walk on, but you know your way around.

Just below the worn steel plate at your feet, the water's calm. Everything looks quiet. No boats in sight. A few people are fishing out their windows. Fish for breakfast? Probably better than meatloaf.

Far over your head, a mag-lev train hums past on a rail bridge. Brine Street's only a few minutes away by train – for rich people living up in the over-city. Not you. Mac once told you that most over-city people never leave the sunny upper levels, and some of them don't even don't know the city's streets are flooded down here. Or don't care, anyway. Maybe that's why there are so many security fences between up there and down here, so that over-city people can pretend that under-city people like you don't exist.

There are fences down here too. To your left, in the

distance, is Big Pig's Wall – a heavy steel mesh fence, decorated with spikes and barbed wire and the occasional skeleton. The same Wall surrounds you in every direction, blocking access above and below the waterline – and Brine Street's on the other side. The extra-dangerous side.

Big Pig's Wall wasn't built to keep people in – no, it's to keep pirates out.

The heavily guarded Tollgates are the only way in or out, and to go through them, everyone has to pay a toll to Big Pig's guards. A dollar per person, more for boats, all paid into big steel-bound boxes marked Donations. Big Pig has grown rich on those "donations". Not as rich as over-city people, but still richer than anyone else in this neighborhood. Some people grumble that Big Pig and his guards are really no better than the pirate gangs, but most locals think the tolls are a small price to pay for some peace and security.

Then again, you happen to know the Tollgates *aren't* the only way in and out – last week, you found a secret tunnel that leads through the Wall. No toll fees if you go that way – two dollars saved. You finger the coins in your pocket.

It's time to make a decision. How will you get to Brine Street? Do you:

Go the longer and safer route through a Tollgate? **P5**
Or
Save time and money, and try the secret tunnel? **P46**

Tollgate

You jog the four blocks to the nearest Tollgate. A surly Gate guard rattles a "donation" box, and you hand over a dollar toll fee.

The gate opens for a boat you know well – the *Rusty Rhino*, an ironclad cargo steamboat with a dozen crew. Looking out over its armored sides is Captain Abdu McCall, wearing his favorite battered red top hat. He waves at you. "Morning, kid. Want a ride? We're headed for Blemmish Market."

The market's only three blocks south of Brine Street – that will save you a lot of walking, and there's no safer way to travel the under-city than on an ironclad.

"Thanks, captain. Great hat."

He smiles, showing all five of his gold teeth. "Another pair of sharp young eyes will be welcome. Pirate trouble's been simmering this last week. Probably just the Kannibal Krew and the Piranhas fighting over their borders, but my left knee's been aching since I woke up this morning, and that's never a good sign."

You don't trust the captain's knee, but you do trust his instincts – he's captained the *Rhino* for years. Maybe this won't be such a safe journey after all. Any pirate gang would love to get their hands on an ironclad.

The *Rhino*'s steam engine chuffs into action, and a sailor hands you a long spear, the same as most of the crew carry. You've never used a spear, and aren't sure whether you could, even to save your own life. Anyway, the spears and other weapons are mostly to scare pirates away. So you stand at the *Rhino*'s side, peer between two armor plates, and try to look fierce.

"How is dear Miss Betty?" Captain Abdu asks. "Still as lovely as ever?"

"Lovely as ever," you agree, trying hard not to giggle. According to rumor, Captain Abdu fell madly in love with Miss Betty twenty years ago. Maybe back then she didn't scowl all the time.

Five minutes later, the *Rhino* passes under a bridge. The crew scan the bridge suspiciously – bridges are a favorite ambush spot for pirates.

Nothing.

"Eyes to port," warns Captain Abdu.

You can never remember the difference between port and starboard, but a red speedboat is approaching at low speed. The driver is a pirate in a skull mask – no, as the boat gets closer, you realize it's a skull tattoo covering his whole head. Next to him is a woman with a Mohawk haircut and a necklace of human teeth. No weapons – well, none in sight.

The speedboat passes the *Rhino*. The pirates wave, grinning unpleasantly.

"A good morning to you," calls Captain Abdu. "You slime-sucking Kannibal Krew scurvy maggots," he adds under his breath.

Surely this can't be an attack – even the Kannibal Krew aren't crazy enough to attack an ironclad with just two pirates – but these two could be scouting before attacking later with bigger numbers. Or maybe they're just going grocery shopping. Either way, the *Rhino*'s crew aren't taking any chances.

The pirate speedboat disappears down a side street. "Good riddance," Captain Abdu mutters.

Half an hour and seven bridges later, just as the *Rhino* turns a corner, the captain kills the engine and sighs.

More pirates? No, a couple of blocks ahead are the flashing blue lights of over-city police hovercraft and jet-skis. Must be something serious – the police never pay much attention to anything happening down here, not unless it affects the over-city too. News drones are buzzing around above crowds of people watching a grey building, as if waiting for something to happen.

"Danger. Please stand back," repeats a voice every few seconds, over a dozen loudspeakers.

The grey building trembles, sways, then collapses in slow motion, and the surrounding block disappears under a huge roaring cloud of dust. The crowd cheer and yell. Some, especially those who were a bit too close, scream and run.

"Wow," says Captain Abdu.

Wow is right. City buildings fall down every year or so – they weren't designed to be up to their ankles in water permanently – but you've never seen it happen before.

"Very entertaining, but now the street will be blocked for weeks while they clear the mess," the captain grumbles. He turns the Rhino and heads south, but the streets are already crowded with boats, barges, canoes and jet skis, some heading towards the blocked street and others headed away, and everyone getting in each other's way. He tries turning east, then west, and shouts and toots the Rhino's steam whistle, but everyone else is shouting and tooting too.

"Can't say when we'll reach Blemmish Market." He looks over at you. "Might be faster to walk to Brine Street. It's up to you."

He's right. It's time to make a decision. Do you:

Stay on the Rhino, even though it might be slower? **P9**

Or

Leave the Rhino, and walk to Brine Street? **P24**

Stay on the Rhino

"I'll stay, thanks," you tell Captain Abdu.

He doesn't notice – he's too busy yelling at someone in a rowboat to get out of the *Rhino*'s way.

Eventually the *Rhino* starts moving again, its steam whistle tooting. The captain shouts so much that he soon sounds hoarse. The *Rhino*'s so slow that you're tempted to leave and walk after all, but the sidewalks are crammed too. Might as well stay on board.

You can't imagine pirates attacking with these crowds around, and you stop checking every single passing boat and bridge, and start daydreaming about what to have for dinner tonight after you've been paid. That's why you don't notice people abseiling down from a bridge onto the *Rhino*'s deck. Black and white striped bandanas cover their lower faces – it's the Piranha gang, the most fearsome slavers in the city. You try to yell a warning to the crew, but you're so scared that only a squeak comes out of your mouth.

One of the Piranhas twirls a baseball bat around her head and steps towards you. Do you:

Use your spear to defend yourself? **P10**

Or

Jump over the side of the boat? **P23**

10

Defend Yourself

You point your spear at the Piranha, but she just laughs and knocks it out of your hands with her baseball bat. She swings it again, this time at your head, and

Everything turns black. **P11**

Boom-boom-boom-BOOM

An elephant's jumping up and down on your forehead – well, that's what it feels like. There must be a huge bruise, you can feel it throbbing in time with your pulse.

So, you're not dead after all. Phew. But your cap's gone. And your backpack and package. And your money.

Above you is a low ceiling of rust-streaked painted steel. You try to sit up, but now a dozen imaginary elephants start jumping up and down.

Captain Abdu looms over you. "Careful, kid, you've been out cold."

He's lost his red top hat. What's that around his wrists…handcuffs?

Oh no. You're wearing them too. So is the crew.

"Where are we?" you croak.

"The cargo hold of the *Rusty Rhino*. The good news is we're all alive, so far. The bad news is we're prisoners on my own boat. Damned Piranhas." He helps you up.

You've never been down here before. The cargo hold has rows of benches bolted to the wooden deck, with an aisle between. The benches are lined up with rows of small holes on each side of the hull. You've seen those holes before from the outside, but never knew what they were – too small to be windows. The holes are no longer empty – each now has a long pole poking through it.

The captain notices your puzzled expression. "We've been drafted as rowing slaves."

Your heart sinks. Looking out the nearest hole, you see that yes, the pole is an oar, its blade high in the air. "Why does a steamboat have oars?"

"I love my dear *Rhino*, but her engine's older than I am, and sometimes we have to row our way home or out of trouble."

"But…I can hear the engine, so why do the Piranhas need us to row?"

He sighs. "We've been wondering the same thing. This isn't the Piranhas' usual way of doing things. They weren't interested in our cargo – threw most of it overboard." A clang and a splash from outside interrupts him. "Hear that? They've been tearing off the *Rhino*'s stern armor plates and tossing them overboard too. Why go to the trouble of hijacking an ironclad, then remove some of its armor, and keep its crew as rowers?"

You try to think, despite your aching head. "They want to lighten the Rhino, but keep its front armor, and they want it as fast as possible, so…so it can ram something, really hard?"

He nods grimly. "That's what we think too. But not if I have any say in the matter. The *Rhino* may be old, but she has some cunning features the Piranhas don't know about. Okay, crew, let's see what we can do." He walks up to the front bench and pokes his fingers under it, and the whole bench hinges up, revealing a box of weapons and tools.

One sailor laughs, but is silenced by the captain's glare.

"We're still outnumbered, outgunned, and locked in," he

says in a low voice. "One false move and the Piranhas will slaughter us." He rummages for a tiny silver tool and hands it to a sailor with a droopy moustache. "Grawlix, you're our best lock picker – get these handcuffs unlocked. But don't take them off – we need to pretend we're still cuffed." He turns to a short brown woman with a tattooed chin. "Crumb, you have the best ears of any of us. Sit yourself by the hatchway and listen for anyone coming. Be ready to raise the alarm with one of your famous sing songs."

She grins.

Grawlix soon has everyone's handcuffs unlocked.

Wondering where the *Rhino* is headed, you watch out the oar hole. Looks like the north end of Beach Road. What's worth ramming around here?

Captain Abdu distributes weapons around the crew. Not to you though. "Sorry, kid, but you're no warrior."

You remember how useless you were with the spear. "I know. When there's trouble, I'm only good at running away."

"That's often the best way to deal with trouble. And we may have need for a fast runner, depending on where the Piranhas are taking the *Rhino*."

"We're on Beach Road. The north end – King Volt's territory. Why, I don't know."

He chews his lip. "Me neither. Money is the only thing the Piranhas care about, and there'd be no profit in ramming one of Volt's power turbines."

The engine noise changes, and the *Rhino* starts to turn.

Crumb bursts into song, in a terrible squeaky voice. Everyone dashes back to their benches, and checks their weapons are out of sight and their handcuffs in place. The captain sits beside you, on a bench on the left side of the boat.

Two sets of footsteps clatter down the stern hatchway.

You glance out the oar hole again. The *Rhino* has stopped, facing south. Due south.

Of course. "They're going to ram Big Pig's Tollgate at the south end of Beach Road," you whisper to the captain.

He raises his eyebrows then nods. "Yes, that could be very profitable," he whispers back, barely audible over Crumb's singing.

A huge woman emerges from the hatchway, followed by a short man wearing spikey shoulder pads and spike-covered gloves, like he's some kind of pirate porcupine. Both have Piranha black and white striped bandanas around their necks.

"Shut up!" the woman yells at Crumb, marches to the front, turns and scowls at everyone. She has muscles on her muscles, and scars galore, and carries a buzzing stun-gun and a mysterious black box. Somehow even her hair – braided with pink teddy-bear ribbons – is scary.

The porcupine man blocks the hatchway steps, the only way out.

"We should have thrown you lot overboard and let the sharks chew on your flabby flesh!" Scary Hair yells. "And maybe we still will. Pick up those oars, or die."

"My crew will follow my orders," Captain Abdu says calmly. "We will row."

You're pretty sure that's his sneaky way of telling the crew to play along for the meantime.

Everyone grabs the oars – even you, although you've never rowed anything bigger than a raft.

"Not as stupid as you look," Scary Hair sneers. "Time to learn my favorite song." She presses a button on the mysterious black box, and a drum beat starts: boom-boom-boom-BOOM-boom-boom-boom-BOOM. For one crazy moment, you think she's going to start dancing or singing, but then realize the 'music' is a rowing beat.

"Pathetic!" she yells at the crew's first rowing stroke. She's right, the timing was terrible – yours especially, losing your grip and hitting your nose on the oar. "Synchronize or suffer!" She points her stun-gun at Grawlix.

The next stroke is better, everyone pushing their oars at nearly the same time, and the third even better. This crew have obviously had plenty of rowing experience together.

Over the drum beat, the *Rhino*'s steam engine chugs at full speed.

Out the oar hole, you see Beach Road whizzing past, faster and faster. The steam whistle blasts warnings every few seconds. There's a scream and a horrible crunch, as someone's boat doesn't get out of the way fast enough, and the Rhino doesn't even slow down. At this rate, you'll be at the Tollgate in minutes.

"Better," Scary Hair barks, marching up and down the

aisle. "Perhaps some of you deserve to live a little longer."

"You know the Pimple?" the captain whispers to you, when she's not looking.

You nod. It's a huge broken concrete column near the Tollgate – people call it the Pimple because of the way it sticks out into Beach Road.

"Our only chance is to ram it," he continues. "Tell me when we're about twenty yards away."

"Less yapping, more rowing!" Scary Hair shouts.

Ram the Pimple? That sounds dangerous, and you have no idea how he'll do it, but you nod anyway.

Out the oar hole, Beach Road races past. Mermaid Street, Ocean View Road, and, wait for it… Armpit Bridge, which means the Pimple's close.

"Now," you shout.

"Hard to port!" Captain Abdu yells.

The whole crew stands. Everyone on the right pushes their oars extra hard. Everyone on the left jams their oars into the water and pulls backwards, you joining in.

The Rhino swerves left. Time seems to slow down. Scary Hair turns and snarls, raising her stun-gun towards the captain. The porcupine man waves his spiked fists in the air. The captain and crew drop their handcuffs and crouch down. Grabbing their weapons? No, grabbing the benches. You do the same, not knowing why.

Crunch! The *Rhino* jolts to a stop, so suddenly that both pirates are thrown to the deck. The *Rhino* crew pile over them. Moments later, Scary Hair stares nervously at her own stun-gun, now pointed at her by Grawlix, and the porcupine man is stuck to the wooden deck by his spiky clothing and two oars.

"No time to waste," the captain tells you. "Run to the Tollgate and raise the alarm."

He and most of the crew swarm up the hatchway. You're close on their heels.

The Piranhas up here on the main deck are still getting back to their feet, with no idea why the *Rhino* crashed into the Pimple. The last thing they expect is for their rowing slaves to burst out of the hatchway, waving weapons.

You dodge a pirate sword, hop over the crushed bow onto the Pimple's concrete, leap down, and race along the Beach Road sidewalk, heading for the Tollgate. "Piranhas!" you yell at the top of your lungs. "Pirate attack! They hijacked the *Rhino* and kidnapped her crew!"

That gets everyone's attention, especially at the Tollgate. Dozens of Big Pig's soldiers dash past you towards the *Rhino*.

The *Rhino*'s crew and the soldiers soon take the Piranhas prisoner, to the delight of the locals – the Piranha gang isn't popular around here.

Captain Abdu, who's somehow found his red top hat again, grins and claps you on the shoulder. "You can't fight and you can't row, kid, but you're quick on your feet. How'd you like to join my crew? Oh, and we found this in the hold." He hands you your backpack. The package is still inside, looking a bit squashed but intact.

It's time to make a decision. Do you:
Join the Rusty Rhino crew? **P19**
Or
Stay a Deadline Delivery courier? **P21**

Join the Rusty Rhino Crew

"Thanks, captain," you say. "I'd love to work on the *Rusty Rhino*."

Of course, it's not quite that simple – the *Rhino*'s still jammed onto the Pimple, with its bow crumpled and leaking.

But word quickly spreads through the under-city about how Captain Abdu's crew outsmarted the Piranha gang and saved Big Pig's territory from invasion. An hour later, Big Pig sends out his best mechanics and boat builders to rescue the *Rhino*. A few weeks later, the boat's been fully repaired. Its new bow is painted with an angry pig logo, signaling to everyone that the boat gets free passage through Big Pig's Tollgates. Forever.

"It's not entirely good news," Captain Abdu admits to you. "When Big Pig does anyone a big favor, he always expects a big favor in return too. But still, we've been attacked by pirates a dozen times before and this time ended better than most. Okay, kid, tomorrow we start our next voyage, transporting rat skins, dried plankton, and jellied eels across the city. Get ready to learn to fight, row, swim, and anything else I can think of."

"Yes, sir!"

Congratulations, this part of your story is over. You have survived a pirate attack and started an exciting new life on board the Rusty Rhino. But things could have gone even better – or even worse. You could have gone up to the over-city, or down to the mysterious domain of the froggies. And there are other pirates down here beside the Piranhas to worry about, like those Kannibal Krew. Or the mysterious Shadows.

It's time to make a decision. Do you:

Go to the list of choices and start reading from another part of the story? **P122**

Or

Go back to the beginning and try another path? **P1**

Stay a Courier

"No, thanks, captain," you say. "I'm not really sailor material. But, um, do you have a spare dollar? I'm broke, dead broke, and can't even pay my toll fee to get back home."

He laughs and gives you twenty dollars. Twenty! Then he hugs you. Half the crew hug you too, until you're blushing.

You wave goodbye, and run to Brine Street – your package delivery is late, and Miss Betty will probably yell at you.

After delivering it, you return to the Tollgate and hold out your dollar toll fee.

"You're that kid," says the guard.

"Um," you say.

"Helped save us from attack by the Piranhas," she says. "Thanks."

"No problem."

"No charge." She waves you through the gate.

Wow, that's never happened before.

Today's turned out pretty well. Twenty bucks in your pocket – enough for dinner and new shoes. Well, not brand-new, but new-ish, the right size and with no holes. Luxury.

You might only be a courier, but life's definitely improving.

Congratulations, this part of your story is over. Even though Miss Betty won't be impressed, helping to defeat a pirate attack was quite an adventure. Although if you'd made different decisions, today could have gone even better – or worse. What if you'd never gone through the Tollgate and caught a ride on the Rusty Rhino at all? Or if you'd left the boat after that building collapsed?

It's time to make a decision. Do you:

Go to the list of choices and start reading from another part of the story? **P122**

Or

Go back to the beginning and try another path? **P1**

Jump Overboard

You run for the side of the *Rhino*, getting ready to jump for your life. But before you can clamber up over the armored side, something hits you on the head, and

Everything turns black. **P11**

Leave the Rhino and Walk to Brine Street

You wave goodbye to Captain Abdu and his crew. "Thanks for the ride."

"Good luck," he shouts, as the *Rusty Rhino* chugs away.

"You too."

Twelve blocks later, near a line of people queuing for who knows what, you find a dented steel door marked with 390 in peeling yellow paint. It doesn't look like much – in fact, you recheck your package's delivery address to be sure this is the address. Yep, 390.

Whatever this place is, they have a serious security system. Cameras watch you, and the door snaps open then shuts itself the moment you've walked through. Inside are white walls and long shelves, ceilings with humming tube lights, and a half-flower half-chemical smell that catches in the back of your throat.

Another smell too – dog, maybe?

A man in a white coat takes the package, scribbles an electronic signature on a data tablet, then walks away, arguing on his phone the whole time and barely looking at you.

Some customers are like that. You don't mind – the worst customers are the ones who blather about nothing for half an hour and make you late for your next job.

The security door lets you out then snaps shut behind you.

So, what now, walk back to Deadline Delivery and hope

Miss Betty has another job for you? Unfortunately, that could mean waiting for hours in the dispatch office, watching her playing Bouncy Bunnies on her computer. But at least there's ten dollars waiting for you back there – that's better than some days.

As you start the long walk back to Nori Street, you have fun imagining the ways you're going to spend that money, starting with a delicious dinner tonight. Just thinking about it makes your stomach rumble happily. You're so busy daydreaming that you don't notice the shadows in an alley, not until they start moving. Too late, you realize they're not shadows but Shadows, the local pirate gang who dress in black from head to toe.

Before you can decide whether it's worth trying to run, something hits you from behind and everything goes dark.

* * *

You wake in the alley, with a throbbing headache. Surprised to be alive, surprised that you still have your clothes, even your cap. Your shoes are gone though. A few yards away is your backpack, slashed open – pointlessly, since it was empty anyway.

Oh. They found the coins in your pocket too, so now you're dead broke. Not even a dollar to get back through a Tollgate. What an awful day.

"Are you okay?" calls a voice.

You look around but can't see anyone.

"Up here."

From far above, an over-city boy looks down through a

security fence.

"I called for an ambulance, but…they said they didn't service lower levels," he continues, sounding confused. "Security reasons, they said."

Stupid over-city kid. Ambulances never come down here, everyone knows that. "Go away," you tell him.

He doesn't. "And then I called the police," he continues. "But I don't think they believed me when I told them three ninjas attacked you."

Huh? "What are ninjas?"

He frowns. "Those guys in black."

"Those were pirates, from the Shadows gang."

He looks even more confused. "Pirates don't dress like that. Pirates wear eye patches and stripy t-shirts and old-timey captain hats. And they have cutlasses and flintlock pistols. And peg legs. And parrots on their shoulders. Well, not all at once, I suppose. And they say 'Arrrrr!' and bury secret treasure and then find it again."

What on earth is he on about? "Go away," you repeat. "I have to walk across town to Nori Street in bare feet, and I'm tired of your stupid over-city babbling."

"Nori Street? That's near where I live. Why don't you catch a mag-lev train? It's only a five-minute ride."

"There aren't any trains down here, dummy. And even if there were, I don't have any money – the Shadows took everything."

"No, I meant the train up here. I'll pay for your ticket. Look here, there's a gap in the security fence where you could squeeze through."

You look up, ready to yell at him, but he's right – about the fence at least – he's flapping a loose section of steel mesh. Just maybe he's not completely crazy.

It's time to make a decision. Do you:

Go up to the over-city? **P28**

Or

No way, you're staying down here. **P38**

Up to the Over-City

"Okay, I'm coming up," you tell the over-city boy.

Easier said than done – you have to climb a slippery concrete wall, then shimmy along a creaking girder, in bare feet. The final part's the worst – clambering hand over hand across heavy steel mesh to where he is. One slip and the thirty-foot fall will probably kill you.

Just as you get there, he holds the mesh closed, blocking your way. "Are you a hooligan or a vagrant?" he asks.

"What?"

"My father says that under-city folk are hooligans and vagrants."

Stupid over-city dad, you want to say but don't, coz you're dangling over a thirty-foot drop, clutching rusty steel mesh that's already digging into your aching fingers. "See my cap? Deadline Delivery, that's the company I work for. I'm just a courier who got mugged by, um, nin joes, like you saw."

"Ninjas," he corrects, then holds the mesh open and lets you swing through. "Hi, I'm Albert."

"I'm, um…Rhino," you lie, trying to rub some feeling back into your sore fingers. No way is he getting your real name.

"Rhino? That's such a cool name, much better than 'Albert'." He points down through the mesh. "Rhino, are they hooligans and vagrants?"

Following his gaze, you see half a dozen people looking

up. "Maybe some of them," you admit. Let's be honest, any route up to the over-city will attract some bad people before long.

Albert puts his thumb to his ear and talks into his little finger. "Hello, I'd like to report a broken security fence. Yes, sending a location-tagged photo now. Thank you." He puts his hand down and looks at you. "They're sending someone immediately."

"You have a phone inside your hand?"

He nods. "I got it for my birthday. I was always losing my phones or forgetting to charge them, this one's so much more convenient. You should get one too, it'd be perfect for a courier."

You laugh. "Sure, after I find one of those pirate secret treasures you were talking about."

"C'mon, Rhino, the next train's in three minutes."

Rhino? Oh, right, he thinks that's your name. Stupid over-city kid.

Maybe it would be safer to leave him and travel alone. But looking around, you feel lost. Even though they're exactly the same streets and buildings, everything up here looks unfamiliar.

So you follow him, shading your eyes. It's so bright – for once there are no security fences between you and the sun. And everything's shiny and clean – buildings, people, everything. The under-city's an almost invisible shadow beneath security fences. No wonder that over-city people forget the under-city even exists.

A hover-van races past and stops where you came through the fence. Two people in overalls leap out, carrying tools.

Albert sighs. "Unbelievable. I report you being mugged down there and no one cares, but…I report a hole in the security fence and they turn up in three minutes flat. It's so unfair."

Maybe he's not so stupid after all. For an over-city boy.

He takes you down the street, past a building which has an entire wall showing a giant video ad for deodorant, to a line of seats which look like they're made of glass (although surely that's impossible). In front of the seats, a gleaming silvery rail continues in both directions down the street – the mag-lev track, and so this must be a train stop, you suppose, but are too embarrassed to ask.

A small train soon approaches. It's shiny and clean, of course, and looks like a spaceship. Albert somehow pays for tickets by wiggling his magic phone-hand again.

"What else can it do? Make coffee?" you ask.

Albert laughs.

From four rows away, two young women turn and glare at you, sniff, and then move further away. Do you stink or something? Yeah, okay, probably. Albert either doesn't notice or is too polite to mention it. He launches into a long story about pirates – his sort of pirates, not the real ones – which makes no sense. Something about walking on a plank and some guy named Jolly Roger.

"Nori Street," a computer voice announces five minutes

later.

One block away is Ivory Tower, although you barely recognize it. This level of the building is covered in marble and chrome and glass, almost beautiful. For a moment, you think you're dreaming and this must be the wrong address. But when you peer down through the security fence, there are the grimy old under-city levels you know so well.

"What's wrong, Rhino?" Albert asks as you cross the street together, on a lacy golden bridge that plays tinkly notes with your every step. Musical bridges – is there anything they don't have up here?

"Just wondering how to get back to the under-city levels."

He frowns, confused again. "Why not use the elevators?"

"Ivory Tower has no elevators on our levels. And the stairwells are blocked, to stop us horrible hooligans and vagrants getting up here." Hmm, wait a minute. Surely the stairwells and elevators must have connected *all* the levels once, back when the building was built, before the city flooded. So…maybe some connections *weren't* blocked?

It's time to make a decision, and fast. Rolling towards you is a police robot, making a grumpy beep-boop-beep-boop noise. Do you:

Go into Ivory Tower? **P32**

Or

Run from the Grumpy Robot? **P35**

Ivory Tower

"I've just had an idea, Albert. It may not work, and it could get me in a lot of trouble, so…goodbye and thanks for all your help."

"Bye, Rhino. Hope I see you again one day." He bends down, takes off his shoes, and gives them to you. "Here, you'll need these, for running away from pirates."

"What?" They're great shoes, so great that you don't want to put them on your dirty feet. You feel a lump in your throat. "Thanks, Albert. They're the best present anyone's ever given me."

He shrugs. "They're just shoes. I've got dozens. Good luck, Rhino."

Clutching the shoes, you sprint up to Ivory Tower's front door before the police robot can catch you.

"Can I help you?" growls a doorman in a fancy uniform, glaring from your grimy bare feet to your dirty Deadline Delivery cap.

You smile at him. "Yes, please. I'm a poor under-city kid who needs to get back to the under-city levels as fast as possible. You want me out of here too, right? So–"

He grabs you by the collar and drags you inside. "How dare you smear your dirty feet over our nice clean floor," he shouts, then adds in a whisper, "Play along for the security cameras. I was born in the lower levels of this very building, and I remember Deadline Delivery. Is Miss Betty still there?" Before you can say a word, he drags you into an elevator and starts shouting again. "We don't want your sort up here, understand, kid?"

Why's he still yelling? Oh, the elevator has a security camera in the corner.

"You're a bunch of dirty, um…"

"Hooligans and vagrants?" you suggest.

"Precisely! Dirty vagrants and hooligans!"

The floor numbers blink down to "8", the doors open, and he pushes you out.

"And don't come back!" As the doors close, you see him wink.

The elevator doesn't even look like an elevator from out here – there are no control buttons, just two stainless steel panels that you know are really its doors. So, it's a one-way elevator – sneaky.

Yes, this really is Level 8 – there's the tattoo parlor at the other end of the corridor, and next to it, Deadline Delivery.

Miss Betty scowls at you, as usual. But she pays you the ten-dollar delivery fee, as promised.

The steel door squeaks and starts to close, and you hurry out. Miss Betty doesn't say goodbye. She never does.

Congratulations, this part of your story is over. You've seen the over-city, and met Albert, who's pretty cool for a crazy over-city kid, and now you have a great new pair of shoes and ten dollars – this is the best day you've had in months.

Would things have worked out so well if you'd made

different choices?

It's time to make a decision. Do you:

Go to the list of choices and start reading from another part of the story? **P122**

Or

Go back to the beginning and try another path? **P1**

Run from the Police Robot

"Goodbye and thanks for your help, Albert. I'd better get out of here before that police robot catches me."

"Wait a moment." He bends down, takes off his shoes, and gives them to you. "Here, you'll run faster in these."

"Really?" They're great shoes, so great that you don't want to put them on your dirty feet. "Thanks, Albert. They're the best present anyone's ever given me." You feel a lump in your throat.

He shrugs. "They're just shoes. I have lots. Good luck, Rhino."

Clutching the shoes, you run down Nori Road.

But the police robot accelerates. Halfway down the block, it catches up and clamps you around the neck with a metal hand. "You are unauthorized," it says, and grabs the shoes with two more hands – it has six hands, at least.

"They're mine, a gift – I didn't steal them," you protest.

"Correct," it says. A little TV screen on its body lights up, and there on screen is Albert giving you the shoes. "You are unauthorized," it repeats, and more pictures appear – you climbing through the security fence, you and Albert catching the train – you've been watched the whole time on security cameras. So much for sneaking around without being noticed.

The robot drags you down an alley, to a large cage labeled Trash.

"I'm not trash!"

"Correct. You are unauthorized," it says again. Robots aren't great conversationalists, that's for sure. It seals the shoes in a plastic bag, and hands them back to you. Huh? "Please hold your breath. Have a nice day." It pushes you into the cage, on top of piles of real trash, closes the door and pulls a lever.

The bottom of the cage swings open.

You fall, screaming.

Just as you hit the water, you remember to hold your breath, even though you can't swim.

But as you splash, you bounce on something. Somehow you're not drowning, you're in a huge rope net stretched over the water. Around you, people sift through all the trash that fell with you.

"Look, it's one of Miss Betty's Deadline Delivery kids," says a man with a dozen earrings.

"Dead?" asks a bald woman. "I know a guy who'll pay ten dollars for dead kids, so long as they're fresh."

"No, still breathing."

"What a shame. Never mind then."

Everyone laughs. You hope they're joking.

"Half a slice of pizza, and the cheese is still soft!" yells the bald woman, swallowing it with a huge smile.

"That's nothing, I found two apple cores!" the man shouts back

Lying beside you on the net is your Deadline Delivery cap. It's soaking wet, like the rest of your clothes (except for Albert's shoes, safe in their plastic bag), but you put it on anyway.

Back at Deadline Delivery, Miss Betty scowls at you, as usual. She pays you the ten-dollar delivery fee, as promised, but only after deducting two dollars as a Wet Uniform fee for your cap. So unfair. You scowl back at her silently.

The steel door squeaks and starts to close, and you hurry out. Miss Betty doesn't say goodbye. She never does.

Congratulations, this part of your story is over. You've seen the over-city, and met Albert, who's pretty cool for a crazy over-city kid.

Even that grumpy police robot was nice to you, in a way.

And now you have a great pair of shoes and eight dollars – this is the best day you've had in months. Would things have worked out so well if you'd stayed in the under-city?

It's time to make a decision. Do you:

Go to the list of choices and start reading from another part of the story? **P122**

Or

Go back to the beginning and try another path? **P1**

Stay in the Under-City

Did that over-city boy really expect you to trust him, a total stranger? Sure, a free train ride home would have been cool, but…he was probably only joking or trying to trick you or something, coz, well, over-city people are crazy. Everyone knows that.

You leave the alley. Where now – home? But how, with no shoes and no money?

Hmm, Beach Road is only a couple of blocks away, and has fairly good footpaths and a Tollgate at its south end. Yeah, heading that way makes sense. As for how to get through the Tollgate without a dollar toll fee…um, you'll think of something. Maybe try that secret tunnel you found on Krill Road last week, although that will mean a lot of climbing over rubble in bare feet.

Twenty minutes later, you've stubbed your toes three times, trodden in dog poop, come within an inch of stepping on a rusty nail, and been sniffed by a hungry-looking cat. Not too much further though – you can see the Beach Road Tollgate in the distance.

A steam engine chuffs behind you, and you turn and see the *Rusty Rhino* ironclad again. Maybe Captain Abdu will give you a ride, perhaps even loan you a dollar for the toll fee.

But…why is the *Rhino* going so fast, and using oars as well as its steam engine? And that's not Captain Abdu at the wheel, although he's wearing the captain's crumpled red top hat. Strange. The captain never ever lets anyone else wear that hat – it's his favorite. Just visible at the guy's neck is a black and white striped bandana – the uniform of the Piranha pirate gang. The *Rusty Rhino*'s been hijacked!

Where are Captain Abdu and his crew? Taken prisoner? Dead?

And where's the *Rhino* going in such a hurry?

You look further up Beach Road and see a line of speedboats are quietly following the *Rhino* at a distance.

You turn the other way and see the Tollgate in the distance. Why isn't the *Rhino* slowing down?

Oh. It isn't speeding *to* the Tollgate, it's going to ram its way *through* the Tollgate. The Piranhas are invading Big Pig's territory!

It's time to make a decision. Do you:

Run to the Tollgate and warn them? **P40**

Or

No, ignore the Rhino. The Tollgate can defend itself. **P44**

YOU SAY WHICH WAY

40

Run to the Tollgate

Is this really a good idea? Outrun a steamboat, in bare feet?

It's not impossible, you tell yourself. The *Rusty Rhino*'s just a slow old cargo boat, even when helped along by oars.

So you start jogging towards the Tollgate.

For the first block, you easily outpace the boat. But then you trip on a loose sidewalk plank and fall, stubbing your toe yet again and scraping your knee.

Ignoring the pain, you get up and carry on running. The *Rhino*'s close on your heels.

Faster.

The Tollgate's just three blocks away.

Two.

One block. The *Rhino*'s catching up.

"Pirate attack!" you yell at the top of your voice. "The Piranhas have hijacked the *Rusty Rhino*!"

Can the guards at the Tollgate hear you yet?

Maybe not, but the people on the street around you can. The locals hate pirates, and hate the slave-selling Piranhas most of all. Some people run off, and others start throwing things at the *Rhino* – stones, bricks, rotten food. Someone even fires an arrow. Not that any of that will do much against an ironclad boat.

The *Rhino*'s chugging alongside you now, and getting faster, or you're slowing down, or both. Onboard, a Piranha glares at you over an armor plate. "I hate loud-mouthed kids," he shouts, and levels a pistol at you. Before he can pull the trigger, a flying brick hits him and he falls, cursing.

Exhausted and out of breath, you stagger to a stop near Armpit Bridge, and shout "Piranha attack!" one last time at the top of your voice.

Just ahead is a huge concrete column, locally known as the Pimple because of the way it sticks out into Beach Road. To your amazement, the oars on the *Rhino*'s left side suddenly jam into the water, and the oars on its right side push extra hard. The boat swerves left, bouncing hard off the Pimple and snapping lots of oars.

How did that happen? It was no accident, you suspect.

The impact has damaged the *Rhino*, and slowed but not stopped it. Its engine's still going and it's speeding up again.

Somehow you find a second wind and dash the rest of the way to the Tollgate, passing the *Rhino* again and hoping no one else takes a pot shot at you. "Pirate attack!"

"Yeah, we heard you the first time, kid," mutters a guard from behind the heavy steel mesh. "Stand back and enjoy the show. Now!" He raises an assault rifle.

You duck into a nearby doorway, wincing at your bruised and bleeding feet, then turn to watch the approaching *Rhino*.

Something whirs and clanks, and five enormous spikes emerge from the water in front of the gate. People on the *Rhino* shout at each other, and the boat tries to turn away. Too late – with a shriek like a dying dinosaur, it collides with the spikes, gouging long holes in its side. Soldiers run out from the Tollgate, and there's more shouting from the *Rhino*.

Only a few shots are fired. Five minutes later, a line of

unhappy pirates are sitting handcuffed on the sidewalk outside the Tollgate.

"Look what those damned Piranhas have done to my poor old boat," says a familiar voice.

It's Captain Abdu on the *Rhino*'s deck, looking down at her ripped and crumpled side. He's reclaimed his red top hat, and that's more ripped and crumpled than usual too.

"Are you and your crew okay, captain?" you ask.

He gives a sad smile. "Thought it was you I heard earlier, shouting pirate attack warnings – thanks for that. We were imprisoned in our own cargo hold, forced to be rowing slaves. A couple of broken bones and a stab wound, but we're all alive and grateful to be so. Could be worse, could be far worse. But I fear the *Rusty Rhino* has made her last voyage."

To everyone's surprise, the captain's wrong.

Big Pig takes the Piranhas' attack on his territory very personally, and has the *Rhino* recovered and repaired, at his own expense. He orders its bow painted with an angry pig logo, signaling to everyone that the boat gets free passage through the Tollgates.

Captain Abdu isn't completely happy about this. "Big Pig just wants to look good to the locals – he'll expect me to pay him back, one way or another. But at least I have my dear old *Rhino* shipshape again."

Somehow Big Pig hears about you too, and orders you to have an angry pig logo tattooed on your hand – that gives you free passage through the Tollgates too. You secretly hate the tattoo, but hey, no more Tollgate fees ever? – that sounds great. Life's definitely improving.

Congratulations, this part of your story is over. You're a hero to most people, except the local pirates. And Miss Betty, who doesn't care about anything except packages being delivered on time, but you don't care about that.

What might have happened if you hadn't raised the alarm about the pirate attack? Or what if you'd never gone up to the over-city at all?

It's time to make a decision. Do you:

Go to the list of choices and start reading from another part of the story? **P122**

Or

Go back to the beginning and try another path? **P1**

44

Ignore the Rhino

The *Rusty Rhino* steams (and rows) past you, followed by half a dozen speedboats, each crowded with people. No weapons are visible, but you spot several black and white striped Piranha bandanas beneath shirts and jackets. Definitely a surprise pirate attack.

Part of you feels guilty, wishing you could do something to warn the Tollgate. But still – outrun a steamboat in bare feet? No way!

Too late now anyway. The pirate fleet has already passed.

Limping, you carry on down Beach Road, watching where you're stepping with your sore bare feet.

There's a huge bang in the distance – either at the Tollgate or close to it – then lots of little bangs. Gunfire? A haze of smoke or dust hides whatever's happening. You keep walking.

Your left foot's bleeding and your right foot has a blister, but you soon forget that as you get closer to the Tollgate – the whole gate's been smashed open. There's no sign of the guards. A body lies face down in the water, and blood stains a sidewalk.

You sneak through the wreckage (not that there's anyone around to hide from) and walk back to Nori Road, detouring each time you hear screams, gunfire, and revving speedboats. There's no other sign of life, except occasional frightened faces peering out from barred windows.

Hearing a throbbing engine, you take cover behind a

smashed crate. A cargo boat goes by, laden with weeping handcuffed people, guarded by grinning Piranhas.

An over-city fire control hovercraft whooshes past. It sprays water over a smoldering boat, then disappears, ignoring you and the slave boat. Typical. Over-city people only care about stopping fires spreading upwards – they couldn't care less what happens to anyone down here.

Getting back to Ivory Tower unseen takes half an hour. You hammer on the bulletproof glass doors. "Let me in!" You can see someone's shadow moving inside, but the doors don't open. "Let me in! I work here."

Someone grabs you around the neck.

"Not any more you don't, kid," a Piranha sneers, and handcuffs you.

I'm sorry, this part of your story is over. You're now a slave of the Piranhas, being herded with dozens of others into a long boat, on your way to…who knows where. If you'd made different choices, things might have worked out better. Or even worse…

It's time to make a decision. Do you:

Go to the list of choices and start reading from another part of the story? **P122**

Or

Go back to the beginning and try another path? **P1**

Secret Tunnel

You climb a creaking fire escape and clamber over the roof of a flooded car salesroom. Through holes in broken skylights, you can sometimes see car skeletons rusting under the water.

You cross a rickety rope suspension bridge, down an alley close to the Wall, and into a small building that everyone ignores because it's covered in bird poop and smells even worse. Then up a staircase with half of its steps missing, then under a broken door. You stop and wait, listening and watching through a hole in a wall, in case anyone's followed you. No point in having a secret tunnel if it doesn't stay secret.

After five minutes, you decide you're alone. There are dog and rat footprints on the dusty floor, but no shoe prints except your own. No other people have been here in a long time. You only found this place last week, completely by accident, while looking for shelter during a rainstorm.

You carry on, through a room lined with shelves of rat-eaten books (and rat nests, judging by the rustling and squeaking) then past a concrete-walled room full of cables, pipes, vents, spider webs and a wall of giant fans. After swinging out the rightmost fan from its frame, you duck into the tunnel behind.

It's only an air duct, and so low you have to crawl on your hands and knees, your backpack scraping along the roof. With every move, the metal walls groan and creak and wobble like they're about to collapse. Don't think about that, keep going, it's worth it, because…

…when you get to the other end, and peer out through a jumble of torn girders, below you is Krill Road. You're through the Wall.

You wait again, watching, listening. Big Pig would be very unhappy if he knew this tunnel existed, and bad things happen to anyone who makes Big Pig unhappy.

Over there, under that floating tangle of blue plastic wrap – is that a pair of eyes looking back at you? No, don't be so paranoid.

Climbing down onto Krill Road, you're watched by a large three-legged ginger cat, but apparently no one and nothing else. The tunnel exit is invisible from here, just a shadow beneath an old upside-down sign advertising hot dogs. Why did people in the olden days always eat their dog sausages in bread rolls?

Everything's quiet. Maybe too quiet. That's always the problem with Krill Road. Long, wide and straight, with good sidewalks and three solid bridges. A great way to get across the city, for people or boats. And the reason pirate gangs like it too.

A line of ducks swims past. Must be safe, right? The ducks seem to think so, and barely glance up as you jog along the top of a crumbling concrete wall on Krill Road's left side.

Suddenly the ducks burst into panicked quacking and take off.

You turn to see a dozen wild dogs trailing you, led by a huge German Shepherd with a ripped left ear.

You know a dog that looks a lot like that. It knows you too, sometimes it even stops and says a doggy hello and you scratch behind its ears. But the dog you know doesn't have a ripped ear. Maybe this is the same dog and it's been in a fight recently, or maybe it isn't the same dog, and you're about to get your throat ripped out. Wild dogs eat almost anything, including kids.

Don't panic. Not yet. Avoiding any sudden movements, you look around, but don't see any ladders or other escape routes where a dog couldn't follow you.

Around a corner chugs a wooden boat loaded high with cabbages. At the boat's center, sitting on a box behind a small steering wheel, is an old woman. There's a sawed-off double-barreled shotgun by her feet.

She smiles toothlessly and slows down. "Jump on, dearie," she says. "You don't look like a cabbage thief. If I see you being eaten alive by dogs, I'll lose my appetite for lunch."

The dogs are getting closer.

It's time to make a decision. Do you:

Accept her offer of a ride? **P49**

Or

Decide not to trust her? **P63**

Cabbage Boat Ride

"Thank you." You climb down into the boat and sit behind the old woman, carefully avoiding cabbages, coiled ropes and an oar.

She revs the engine and the boat burbles off, to howls of disappointment from the dogs.

Something splashes nearby. No, not a dog, just a huge rat swimming past, perhaps escaping the dogs too. Another splash, a flicker of too many teeth, and the rat's gone, leaving only ripples. A shark? People claim there are crocodiles and giant octopuses prowling the flooded streets too. Or maybe it was froggies – the green-skinned mutant people who live underwater and snatch at anything and anyone on the surface. Not that you've ever seen a froggy, but everyone says it's true.

The dogs are soon out of earshot, but a few minutes later something else can be heard over the engine's burbling – a high-pitched roar, getting louder. Looking back, you see a blood-red speedboat approaching. On both sides of the road, people disappear behind doors and slam windows shut.

"Pirates!" yells the old woman, glancing back too. "Looks like the Kannibal Krew. So sorry, dearie." Everyone knows the Kannibal Krew really are cannibals.

"Not your fault." You grab the oar and start paddling. Every little bit helps, right?

She laughs sadly. "That's very sweet of you, dearie, but

this old tub can't outrun a speedboat."

You scan both sides of the road, looking for somewhere safe to leap out.

The cabbage boat swerves around a corner, and the old woman cuts the engine.

"What are you doing? This is a dead end!"

She points her sawed-off shotgun at you. "Yes, I know, dearie. Drop the oar. Like I said, I'm so sorry, but the Kannibal Krew and I have an arrangement – I hand over any passengers to them, and in return they don't eat me."

"That's not fair!"

"Not for you, perhaps, but it's a pretty good deal for me. And you should know not to accept lifts from strangers."

"Look behind you. We're going to crash."

She sneers. "I'm not falling for that old trick – do you think I was born yesterday?"

The drifting boat really is about to collide with the side of the road. You have seconds to make a decision. Do you:

Jump out of the cabbage boat? **P51**

Or

Stay on the boat, jumping looks too dangerous? **P61**

Jump out of the Boat

With a bang, the cabbage boat hits a brick pillar on the side of the road, tipping the old woman onto the cabbages. Before she has time to recover, you leap off the boat and scramble onto the sidewalk, dodging from side to side to spoil her aim.

She yells some very rude words. Her shotgun blasts, and something stings your back.

It hurts, but you're still alive, so you keep running, and flee up a flight of worn steps that lead you don't know where. You randomly turn left and right half a dozen times, then fall in a heap behind a low wall, exhausted and gasping for breath and completely lost.

But safe. For the moment.

You check your stinging back. Just two shotgun pellet wounds and a little blood – you were lucky, very lucky. You can feel one pellet under your fingertips and dig it out, wincing in pain. The other's in too deep and hurts too much. Worry about it later.

Your backpack was hit too. What about the package inside? Pulling it out, you see three small holes and hear broken glass tinkling. Oh no. Miss Betty won't be pleased. Although…why isn't the package leaking more? A large broken bottle would be dripping everywhere, but this, there's just a little dampness and a weird sour smell. Not booze – that's a relief, you'd hate to have risked your life just so some rich person can get drunk.

You peer over the low wall. Carefully, in case any old women with shotguns are looking for you. Or pirates. Or anyone else.

Several blocks to the north is a tall green building you recognize – it's only a block from Brine Street, so you're closer than you'd expected. Maybe that old woman did you a favor after all.

Things are peaceful enough – people hanging washing from lines at windows, small children playing and arguing.

You make your way down to the street, ignoring two yapping skinny puppies. There's no sign of pirates or cabbage boats, so you jog north.

Two blocks later, you find a market you've never seen before, spread over the roof of a low building. Rows of stallholders are selling oily engine parts, electrical junk, toys, weapons, food, and all sorts of stuff. None of it's any good to you, not with only a dollar in your pocket. Ignoring the delicious smell of barbequed rat, you carry on.

Brine Street, at last. Most of the addresses aren't numbered, and it takes you a while to find the steel door marked 390 in peeling yellow paint. There's a long line of people queuing along the sidewalk, you don't know why – they're definitely not queuing for 390. Some of them pretty scary-looking. Nearly as scary as the three security guards, stomping around and keeping order with stun-guns.

You try to edge past the crowd, towards 390.

A man yells at you – maybe he thinks you're queue-jumping – and someone else joins in, and suddenly everyone's pushing and shoving and shouting. Then just as suddenly, everyone stops and backs away and pretends you're not there.

A security guard looms over you, his buzzing stun-gun in hand. "Where do you think you're going, kid? You steal that cap?"

"No, sir, I have a delivery for 390 Brine Street," you squeak, unzipping your backpack.

Without asking, he grabs the package and stares at it, then drags you over to the yellow door, hands you back the package, bangs on the door and walks away.

Huh?

A security cam swivels down at you. The door rolls open, then snaps shut the moment you're through.

What is this place? Lots of white walls and shelves, suspiciously clean, ceilings with quietly humming tube lights, and a half-flower half-chemical smell that catches in the back of your throat.

A huge grey dog shuffles towards you. He has no back legs, just two wheels held on with a frame of metal rods and leather straps. But even so, you're pretty sure he could eat you alive if he wanted to.

"Nice doggy," you stammer.

He sniffs at you suspiciously, and says, "Wuff."

A tired-looking woman in a white coat and a bulletproof vest marches through a doorway and snatches the package from you. She slices the plastic wrapping with a scalpel, revealing a Styrofoam box full of finger-sized bottles. "What happened?" she asks, holding up a broken bottle.

Oh no. Miss Betty deducts fees for any breakages, no matter whose fault they are.

"Shotgun blast. A couple of pellets hit me too."

"Show me," she orders.

None of her business, but she's still holding that scalpel and it looks really sharp, so you show her the two small bloody patches on your back.

She grunts, as if reluctantly believing you.

"What's in those tiny bottles?" you ask, even though it's none of your business – if she can ask nosey questions, then so can you, right?

"Drugs."

You choke. "I'm a drug smuggler?"

She laughs. "*Medical* drugs. To be precise, antibiotics, one week past their expiry date. They were donated to us by a wealthy over-city hospital across town – we need all the help we can get. I'm Doctor Hurst, and this is the Brine Street Community Medical Clinic. A shame that one bottle got broken, but there's enough left to treat half of the people queuing outside our main entrance next door. You want me to fix up those shotgun wounds?"

Is this really a medical clinic? The closest to a clinic you've ever seen is old Charlie on Level 6 of Ivory Tower – he charges a bottle of moonshine whiskey to stitch up any wounds, uses half of it to sterilize the wounds and drinks the other half while he's stitching. He's better than nothing, but not much.

"Um, okay," you say, deciding to trust Doctor Hurst. Well, she does look…doctory. And doesn't smell of whiskey.

It only takes her a few minutes to dig out the other shotgun pellet – which hurts, but not too badly. The dog sniffs you again, and licks your hand. Maybe it's being nice, or maybe it's tasting you.

The doctor dabs something purple on both wounds. "You were lucky, they're just flesh wounds. Keep them clean and dry and they'll heal fine." She walks over to a desk and types on a computer keyboard. The Deadline Delivery web site appears on screen, and she presses the green Delivery Received icon. "I won't mention the one broken bottle."

"Thank you. Thanks so much."

The doctor looks you up and down, and frowns. "How much do you make for a delivery like this?"

Another nosy question, but you answer anyway. "Ten dollars."

"No wonder you're so skinny. That's terrible – we pay the delivery companies far more than that, but you kids take the risks. Wait a minute, I've got an idea." She leaves through a door.

You can hear her arguing with someone, but not what they're saying.

"Wuff," says the dog, sniffing your trousers.

"Nice doggy," you repeat nervously.

He grins, showing lots of teeth and a long tongue, and says, "Wuff" again.

Oh, he can smell your leftover meatloaf from breakfast. You'd planned to keep it for lunch, but…never mind. You pull the plastic bag from your pocket, and share the meatloaf with him.

He swallows it in one bite, then licks your face. "Wuff, woof."

"You're welcome." You scratch behind his ears.

A few minutes later, Doctor Hurst returns. "How'd you like a permanent job as our clinic courier? It'll be hard work, and dangerous, but no more than what you do now, and you'll be better paid. And better fed."

No more working for Miss Betty? Hmm, that sounds good…but what do you really know about the Brine Street Community Medical Clinic?

It's time to make a decision. Do you:

Take the job? **P113**

Or

Think about it and decide later? **P57**

Decide Later

"Um," you say. "Can I think about it?"

"Sure, no rush," says Doctor Hurst. "Where are you going now?"

"Back to Deadline Delivery in Nori Road for my next delivery job."

"That's a rough neighborhood," she says.

"Yeah, but so is Brine Street."

She grins. "True. How'd you like an easy delivery job on your way back? 157 Nori Road. Twenty dollars, in advance."

"Okay," you say, before she can change her mind. Twenty dollars is heaps, and 157 is inside the Wall, only a block away from Ivory Tower. Easy money.

She hands you a small heavy box and the money.

You say goodbye to her and the two-legged dog, and leave.

Outside, the queue of clinic patients is even longer than before. Most of the people ignore you – you're just some boring courier coming out a boring yellow door – but a few stare, including a scary-looking woman with a Mohawk haircut and a necklace of teeth. A pirate, maybe? She's carrying a baby, and the baby stares at you too.

You pretend to ignore them, but the woman turns and whispers to an old man with his beard in dreadlocks and red beads.

Trouble?

That's the problem with wearing a Deadline Delivery cap

– every few months, someone tries to rob you, even though the stuff you carry is hardly worth stealing. But Miss Betty insists all her couriers have to wear the stupid caps, and somehow she knows if anyone doesn't.

At the end of the block, you glance back ever so casually, and sure enough, the old man's following you, his red beaded beard glinting in the sun.

You're not worried. Not yet. You know this part of the under-city well. At the next alley, you turn left, still walking slowly. As soon as you're hidden by the building walls, you dash down the alley, turn left through an archway, and keep running. You dodge through the second-right doorway, down another alley, up a ladder, along the top of a wall, then jump down the other side and back onto the road, and stop, out of breath.

Hiding your cap in your backpack, you check in both directions. No sign of the old man.

Okay, back to Nori Road.

Easier said than done. Four blocks later, you turn left and find the whole road ahead blocked by a collapsed building. Must have just happened – there are still clouds of dust everywhere. Over-city police hovercraft and ambulances and news drones buzz around, a team of giant rescue robots lift girders and concrete beams, and of course a zillion people are watching. You'll never get through this way, not for hours, perhaps days.

So you turn right and detour around several blocks, hiding or changing direction whenever you spot suspicious people or boats.

Unfortunately, that all takes time, and hours pass before the Wall comes into view again. Your feet ache, and so do your shotgun wounds.

There's the hot dog sign up ahead. Not far now.

You stop. Something's different.

Oh. The sign – before, it was upside-down, but now it's more…sideways.

Has someone else found the secret tunnel?

Staying out of sight as much as possible, you get closer.

A hand clamps down on your shoulder. It's the old man with the dreadlocked beard. "You're a sneaky dodgy twisty-turny wee thing, that's for sure. Dragging me halfway across the city, when all I want is a nice wee chat. Young people today – so rude. Now, I can't help but notice your interest in this here wall of junk." He smiles, revealing shiny metal teeth. "That seems a remarkable coincidence, because I hear that just a few hours ago some of Big Pig's crew were also terribly interested in this very same wall. Spent two hours hammering and welding, they did, and then went away, without a word of explanation. Quite a puzzle. Although by another remarkable coincidence, we're right by the Wall, aren't we? And what with you being a courier, and needing to get through the Wall so often…ah yes, I see by your eyes that I guessed right. Well now, losing that wee secret door is a shame for both of us, to be sure. We in the Kannibal Krew are also fond of having a few hush-hush ways of getting from here to there and there to here, yes, indeed." His smile widens, as though this is some huge joke.

A blood-red speedboat approaches, driven by the woman with the Mohawk. Next to her is a bald man with a skull tattoo covering his head. He's holding the same baby you saw outside the clinic. It stares right at you, same as before. Eying you up as lunch, perhaps.

"Let's go for a wee trip," the old man says, and nudges you towards the boat. For a moment, his grip on your shoulder weakens. This could be your only chance. Do you:

Try to run from the Kannibals? **P114**

Or

Follow the old man's orders? **P117**

Stay on the Boat

The collision rocks the cabbage boat to one side, and the old woman overbalances, her shotgun waving wildly. You dive flat onto the hull – not that a pile of cabbages will protect you. The shotgun blasts over your head, so close that you're amazed to still be alive.

Looking up, you glare at her. "I told you we were going to crash."

She snorts and spits into the water. "Right little smarty-pants, aren't you, dearie? Fat lot of good it's done you – or will do, for what's left of the rest of your short life."

You sit up – slowly, because she's pointing the shotgun at you again. The side of your head hurts, and something's dripping down your face. Blood. You take off your *Deadline Delivery* cap and see two small bloody holes.

"Don't cry," she says with a sneer. "You won't bleed to death. Well, not from that."

Huh? Oh, of course, the pirates. The red speedboat swirls to a stop in front of the cabbage boat, blocking the road and your last hope of escape.

In the speedboat are two pirates – a bald man with a skull tattoo covering his head, and a woman with a Mohawk haircut. Both wear necklaces of human teeth. "Lunch!" they roar, grinning at you. They're not talking about the cabbages.

The man leaps onto the cabbage boat, giggling and waving a huge machete.

You scream. The last thing you ever see is that machete,

glinting in the sun as it whooshes down towards you.

I'm sorry, this part of your story is over. You weren't careful enough in this dangerous city, so you died. Perhaps things would have gone better if you'd made some different decisions... and lucky you, you can try again.

It's time to make a decision. Do you:

Go to the list of choices and start reading from another part of the story? **P122**

Or

Go back to the beginning and try another path? **P1**

No Cabbage Boat Ride

"No, thank you," you tell the old woman politely, keeping an eye on her hands. You know better than to trust a free ride from just anyone in the under-city.

Sure enough, she reaches down for her sawed-off shotgun.

You run, heading for the only nearby cover, a collapsed brick wall. Just as you duck around a doorway, the shotgun booms and the top of the doorframe disintegrates into splinters.

She yells some very rude words – well, some of them you haven't heard before, but they definitely sound rude. The shotgun booms again and you're showered in brick dust. She knows where you're hiding, and there are no easy ways out of here.

At least the gunshots have scared those wild dogs away.

You hear a speedboat approaching, then the woman arguing with someone. Sneaking a glance around the doorway, you see a blood-red speedboat with two pirates on it. Kannibal Krew, most likely – one is bald, with a skull tattoo over his whole head, and the other has a Mohawk haircut. Both wear strings of teeth around their necks.

"There!" the old woman yells, pointing straight at you.

Whoops. No time to lose, no time even to think. The only thing that matters is getting away, and fast. You run, ducking and dodging from side to side, not knowing where you're going.

Another shotgun blast, but nothing hits you. Hopefully you're out of range.

The pirates are a bigger worry than the old woman. No way can you outrun a pirate speedboat – your only hope is to go somewhere they can't follow.

You sprint towards an open door, but someone slams it shut and locks it before you get there. Can't blame them – everyone's scared of the Kannibal Krew.

Racing around a corner, you look for a half-remembered alleyway, but it's not there – oh, right, you're thinking of a different road, three blocks away. No useful doorways, ladders, or stairways are in sight. The speedboat revs, getting closer. The pirates have spotted you.

You dash over a bridge and around another corner. The water's covered in floating trash here, and it's nearly low tide. Soon, some of these streets will be little more than deep sticky mud. Enough to clog a speedboat engine or strand the whole boat.

Apparently the pirates think the same – their speedboat slows, and the tattooed man clambers up to the bow and pokes a long pole into the floating trash, probably checking whether it's water or mud underneath. But the boat's still moving, still getting closer. From behind its wheel, the Mohawked woman waves at you and laughs like a hyena.

Through a broken wall, you spot a concrete stairwell leading upwards. No idea where it goes, but it's got to be safer than here. You run up the stairs – as quietly as possible, in case the Kannibals give chase.

At the top of two long flights of stairs is another level with broken walls. A pathway's been cleared through the rubble, to a narrow footbridge stretching over the street. Just what you need, except a group of people are blocking the way – they're crouched by a nearby wall, peering down at the street below. They're wearing black and white striped bandanas – the uniform of the Piranha pirate gang, the worst slavers in the city.

Heart pounding, you duck behind a pillar, hoping they haven't noticed you.

No, they're too busy watching the street and arguing.

"How about that boat there?" one grumbles, pointing down. "An adorable family with four little kids and no weapons. Easy pickings. Little kids sell for fifty bucks at the moment – more if they're cute."

"No, we don't want no adorable families, not today. The boss wants an ironclad boat," says another.

"Don't see why. Ironclads have heaps of armed guards. Risky target, very risky. What's he want an ironclad for?"

"How would I know? Sunday afternoon visits to his dear old mum, maybe. Some new special sneaky plan, that's all I've heard. I just do what I'm told, and so should you."

From the shadow of the pillar, you take a longer look. Six Piranhas, wearing harnesses, and with coils of rope at their feet – they must be planning on attacking a boat by abseiling down from the bridge.

The grumbly pirate has a good point – why go to the trouble of attacking an ironclad boat? The only ironclad you know is the *Rusty Rhino*, a cargo steamboat with a well-armed crew who'd have no trouble fighting off half a dozen Piranhas.

From behind you, clattering up the staircase, come two sets of footsteps – probably the Kannibal Krew searching for you.

Pirates in front, pirates behind. Big trouble. Then again, the Kannibal Krew and Piranhas hate each other – that could help you.

It's time to make a decision. Do you:

Make a run for the bridge? **P67**

Or

Stay where you are, and hope the pirates fight each other? **P85**

Make a Run for the Bridge

"Kannibal Krew! Help!" you yell, running towards the footbridge.

Not that you expect the Piranhas to help you on purpose. And they don't – exactly as you'd hoped, they charge at the surprised-looking Kannibals instead.

Perfect. You dash over the narrow bridge, feeling clever.

But as you reach the other side, a foot stretches out and sends you sprawling across a dusty floor.

A dozen more Piranhas surround you. Oh, of course, they were hiding on *both* sides of the bridge. And you've spoiled their ambush. No wonder they're angry.

One of them knocks your Deadline Delivery cap to the floor, and rips your backpack off. "A courier?" He grins nastily. "You're lost, kid. Dangerously lost. This is a bad part of town."

"Grinder's signaling us," says a scarred woman, looking over the bridge. "They got Kannibal Krew trouble."

Most of the Piranhas lose interest in you and dash over the bridge, yelling and waving weapons.

"Kill the kid. We don't want no witnesses," the scarred woman says to the man rummaging in your backpack, then sprints after the others.

The man pulls out the package and reads the label. His nasty grin turns…almost nice. "390 Brine Street? They've sewed me up often enough. It's your lucky day, kid – I won't kill you this time. Get out of here before I change my mind." He tosses you your backpack and package and disappears over the bridge, leaving you alone and confused. Who sewed him up? What's at 390 Brine Street?

Whatever. Those Piranhas could return at any moment, so you run out the door in the opposite wall.

This building's stairwells are mostly blocked or missing, so finding another way out is hard work. Eventually you decide to squeeze through a broken window, trying not to break any more of its jagged glass in case the noise attracts attention.

You make it through with just one long scratch, then notice a bloodstained green plastic card on a lanyard, lying amongst the broken glass on the floor. Looks familiar – where have you seen those cards before? Oh yeah, it's a security pass for day workers going up to the over-city.

On its other side is the name Ortopa Baskirl, whoever he or she is. Or was – that's probably Ortopa Baskirl's blood on it.

You're soon back down on the streets and on the way to Brine Street again, but you keep looking up at the over-city and fingering Ortopa Baskirl's security pass in your pocket. Could you use it yourself? You've always wanted to see the over-city with your own eyes, not just from through a security fence or on television.

Ten minutes later, you're at 390 Brine Street, and deliver the package to some grumpy guy who's in too much of a hurry (or too snooty) to say "hello" or "thank you". You hardly notice, still thinking about the over-city.

A couple of blocks away, you pass one of the long ladders which go up to the over-city. They're fenced off and guarded, of course – over-city people don't want under-city people sneaking up there and getting up to no good. A dozen day workers queue at the ladder's bottom, wearing green security passes just like the one in your pocket.

It's time to make a decision. Do you:

Pretend the security pass is yours, and join the queue of day workers? **P70**

Or

Try to return the security pass? **P82**

Pretend the Security Pass is Yours

You stuff your Deadline Delivery cap into your backpack, slip the security pass lanyard around your neck, and join the line of day workers. A couple of them glance at you, but don't say anything.

As each worker reaches a steel gate at the front of the queue, they swipe their pass past a glowing green light, and the gate says "hello" and the person's name in a cheerful computerized voice, and then lets that person through.

When it's your turn, you swipe your pass the same way, ready to run if alarm bells ring, but the gate just cheerfully says, "Hello, Ortopa Baskirl," and opens. More people are already queuing behind you, so you go through the gate, keeping your head down.

Stairs. Hundreds of stairs, all the way up to the over-city. And at the top, there's another queue at another security gate.

"You're not Ortopa Baskirl," says a voice behind you.

Uh-oh. You turn and see an olive-skinned man with no eyebrows.

"Ortopa's sick today, so I'm doing his job for him," you say. Not a very convincing lie, but it's the best you can think of.

Mister No-Eyebrows raises his non-existent eyebrows. "Really? Strange, coz Ortopa's a woman – we work together. I don't know or care who you are, kid, but you'd better be a hard worker, or else."

"I am a hard worker. Um, working at what?"

He doesn't answer.

The security gate lets you through, and you get your first proper view of the over-city. Everything's shiny and clean, and so bright it hurts your eyes, although maybe that's just because up here the sunlight doesn't have to filter down though security fences. All the over-city people look shiny and clean too, just like on television. They ignore you and the other day workers, as if you're invisible.

Mister No-Eyebrows leads you a few blocks away to a tall building, and you both enter through a narrow side door, after swiping your passes again. He pushes you down a carpeted corridor and through several more doors (swiping passes each time) then into a room full of mirrors and tiles. He hands you a pair of purple gloves and a bucket full of plastic bottles and clean rags. "Okay, show me how hard you can work."

Looking around, you realize this must be a bathroom, although nothing like any in the under-city – down there, you hold your breath and get out as fast as possible, hoping there aren't too many cockroaches and rats in there with you. If you can find a bathroom. This bathroom...well, those shiny things must be taps, but why are there five of them? And why does this place need cleaning anyway? – it's the cleanest room you've ever seen. But he's watching you, so you put on the gloves, then mop and scrub and wipe and polish everything in sight.

"Mmm," he says, unsmiling. "A bit slow, but not bad for

a first try. Next."

Next what?

He leads you along a corridor to…another bathroom, like the first except this one is pale pink and has gold taps. Solid gold? Who knows – over-city people are crazy.

"Well, what are you waiting for?" he asks. "We've got eighty-three more to do today."

Eighty-three? Sighing, you pick up your sponge again.

This time he helps, showing you a faster way to mop the floor, and a trick for polishing taps.

Eighty-two to go. The next one is pale blue, with butterflies painted across the ceiling. Pretty, although not much fun to clean.

And so on, bathroom after bathroom after bathroom, with just one short lunch break, hours later – thankfully not in a bathroom.

Mister No-Eyebrows never tells you his name, and calls you "Fake Ortopa". The only things he ever talks about are cleaning-related – stain removal, the best way to polish mirrors, and unblocking clogged drains.

By the end of the day, your hands ache, your back hurts, and you've got a weird itchy rash on your left wrist. Today wasn't what you'd expected from your first visit to the over-city – you now know more than you ever wanted to about fancy bathrooms. All you saw of the rest of the over-city was a few glances out windows.

"Good work today, Fake Ortopa," Mister No-Eyebrows says, as you return to the over-city street level together.

"You scrub toilets better than the real Ortopa, and that's what matters to me. Back tomorrow?" He swipes his card.

"Maybe." Is scrubbing toilets better than working as a courier? Depends – are you going to get paid for today, and how much? Or does he love cleaning so much that he does it for free, and expects you do the same?

You swipe your card, the door opens and you walk out, straight into the arms of a burly security guard. "Ortopa Baskirl?" she asks, grabbing your security pass lanyard and almost choking you with it.

"Um, yeah?" you squeak.

She grins like a shark. "Really? Ortopa Baskirl was found floating face-down in an under-city street this morning." She turns to Mister No-Eyebrows. "You. Scram!"

He does.

"I found Ortopa's pass by accident," you babble to the guard. "I don't know anything about her, or her death. It was probably the Piranha gang, but…"

"Shut up." She drags you over to a gleaming dark green luxury car hovering a few inches in the air.

From its open rear window, a well-dressed man smiles at you. "You're in a lot of trouble, kid. Trespassing, possession of stolen property, identity fraud, interfering with murder evidence," he says, counting each point on his fingers. Then he opens the car door. "Or this could be the best day of the rest of your life."

Who is this guy? No matter how much trouble you're in, you don't trust him one bit. No way do you want to get in this car – but the guard just picks you up, tosses you inside then slams the door.

The guard gets into the front seat and the car glides away so silently you wouldn't know it was moving if the street outside wasn't sliding past.

"Relax, kid, enjoy the ride," the man says, still smiling. "I'm Bradley Lime, recruitment specialist for the Avocado Corporation – I'm sure you've heard of us." You shake your head but he doesn't notice and keeps talking. "I've been watching you on security camera footage, deciding what to do with you. Naturally, under-city people try to sneak up here every day. Most of them want to steal something or smash something or hurt someone, or all three. Can't have that now, can we? No, the nice folks up here want peace and quiet, law and order, not a bunch of dirty under-city hooligans running around. But you, you sneaked up here and …spent the day cleaning bathrooms. Interesting."

Wasn't my idea, you feel like saying, but don't.

Bradley's still smiling like a toothpaste ad. "The Avocado Corporation thinks disadvantaged kids deserve a chance for a successful life here in the over-city, so we're offering you a job as trainee manager. All expenses paid, including food, accommodation, and uniform."

The car stops, next to a forest building – a skyscraper covered in plants and trees and flowers. You've seen them before, looking up from the under-city, but never up close like this.

"You'd be working here, at Avocado Corporation Urban

Organic Farm number 29," he continues. "What do you say, kid?"

You don't understand half of what he's said. Some sort of job here in the over-city. That sounds good, but…what's an urban farm? And what does a trainee manager do, and what do they get paid?

It's time to make a decision. Do you:

Take the job, because it has to be better than being a courier? **P76**

Or

Say no, and get away from this crazy guy as soon as you can? **P79**

Avocado Corporation

"Okay," you say to Bradley Lime, and try to smile.

But you can't compete with his grin, which just got even wider. "Best of luck, kid."

The guard takes you into the "urban farm" building, through a door labeled *Management Only*, and slams the door shut, leaving you inside. You try the door, but it's locked.

It's a strange room, hot and humid. The walls are thousands of small panes of glass, and through them is nothing but green – endless rows of plants and trees. Oh, the whole building must be full of plants. Yeah, an urban farm, that makes sense now. Places like this must be where farmers grow food for over-city people.

"What do you want?" asks a voice behind you.

Turning, you see a sweaty young woman in a green Avocado Corporation t-shirt.

"Um, hi, I'm your new trainee manager," you say.

"No one tells me anything." She sighs and taps on a tablet computer. "Oh, right. Lucky you. Hi, I'm Marcie, junior assistant manager, welcome to your exciting new career at the Avocado Corporation." Marcie sure doesn't sound excited. "Follow me. I'll get you a t-shirt – they must be worn at all times. Corporate policy. And you'd better watch the New Employees video. Corporate policy."

Over the next few hours, you hear "corporate policy" about a million times from Marcie. Apparently the Avocado Corporation has rules for absolutely everything.

Then it's dinnertime in the Avocado Corporation staff cafeteria. There's plenty of food and it tastes okay, and you eat until you're stuffed. But you don't enjoy it much – sitting at the same table are eleven other trainee managers, and they're the glummest people ever. So far, the only happy Avocado Corporation employee you've met was Bradley Lime. Maybe he wasn't really smiling, maybe he was just showing his teeth. Or maybe it's against corporate policy for trainee managers to smile or laugh.

Marcie looks at her watch. "Evening shift starts in three minutes. Follow me," she tells you.

Maybe now you'll finally find out what a trainee manager does around here.

She takes you up and down stairs and along glass-walled corridors, stopping now and then to check numbers on computer screens – humidity, temperature and so on. Despite the zillion plants on the other side of the glass, you haven't touched one leaf yet. Who's doing the weeding and planting and harvesting? Robots?

Then you see movement through the glass – people trudging along, carrying trowels and baskets. They look even sadder than the trainee managers, and aren't wearing Avocado Corporation t-shirts. Hey, one of them is Mac, the owner of Mac's Greasy Spoon back at Ivory Tower! What's he doing here? Behind them swaggers a man wearing a Piranha black and white striped bandana and carrying a stun-gun in his meaty hand.

All of a sudden, everything makes horrible sense.

"They're slave workers, aren't they? The Piranha gang supplies the Avocado Corporation with slaves to do the farm work."

Marcie rolls her eyes. "Duh! This farm has to supply nine thousand lettuces and three thousand cucumbers by 4 am tomorrow morning. Who do you think's going to do all that work? Better them than us. Behave yourself, or you'll end up as one of them – that's corporate policy."

I'm sorry, this part of your story is over. You've made it up to the over-city, discovered the Avocado Corporation's terrible secret and what happens to the Piranha gang's slaves. Working as a trainee manager is going to be awful, no matter how much they feed you and pay you – you don't want to have anything to do with slavery. Life was so much simpler back in the under-city – if only you hadn't taken that security pass…

It's time to make a decision. Do you:

Go to the list of choices and start reading from another part of the story? **P122**

Or

Go back to the beginning and try another path? **P1**

Get Away from Bradley Lime

"Thanks anyway, but I don't think I'd be a good trainee manager," you tell Bradley politely.

His smile disappears. "I guess you're not so smart after all."

The guard opens the car door, and she drags you over to the urban farm building. You struggle, but she's too strong. Without a word, she shoves you through a door labeled *Staff Only*, then slams it shut, leaving you inside.

You try the door, but it's locked.

What is this place? There are plants absolutely everywhere, in pots and on racks along the walls. Some are vegetables and fruits, but others you don't recognize. The air is hot and humid. Bright too – the walls are thousands of small panes of frosted glass. Above, instead of a ceiling, there's a layer of steel mesh, and above that, more plants. Hmm, maybe the whole building's nothing but plants on every level? Yeah, an urban farm, that makes sense now. Places like this must be where farmers grow food for over-city people.

But why did the guard put you here? Will you be forced to become a trainee manager after all?

From behind a tree walks Mac, the owner of Mac's Greasy Spoon back at Ivory Tower. You stare at each other in surprise.

"So they got you too, huh?" he asks. "At least you're alive – we lost some good people today."

"What are you talking about? What are you doing up here, Mac?"

"What are *you* talking about?"

"What?"

"Stop saying 'what'. How did you get here, kid? Weren't you caught in the raid with the rest of us?"

"What raid?"

"You really don't know?" He sighs. "The Piranhas hijacked an ironclad boat and rammed one of Big Pig's Tollgates. They grabbed a hundred or so people, killing anyone who resisted, then brought us back here."

Oh no. You overheard those Piranhas talking about hijacking an ironclad – they must have wanted it for the raid.

He frowns. "So how did you end up here?"

"Um, well, pirates were involved, but...it's a long story. Believe it or not, I've spent most of today cleaning over-city toilets."

"Back to work, lazy scum," yells a sour-faced woman holding a whip. She has a black and white striped bandana around her neck.

"What are Piranhas doing up here in the over-city?" you whisper to Mac as you follow him down a long tree-lined passage.

"The Piranhas supply slave labor to the Avocado Corporation, of course. You don't think over-city people dirty their own fingers weeding lettuces and picking tomatoes, do you?"

"Maybe we could smash a window and escape?"

He snorts. "Look at those little windows, surrounded by those solid steel window frames. This is a prison, and there's no escape. We're slaves, kid. For the rest of our lives."

I'm sorry, this part of your story is over. Trusting Bradley Lime was a big mistake – clearly, the over-city's just as dangerous as back in the under-city. What might have happened if you'd stayed down there? Or escaped the pirates earlier? Or not gone through the secret tunnel at all?

It's time to make a decision. Do you:

Go to the list of choices and start reading from another part of the story? **P122**

Or

Go back to the beginning and try another path? **P1**

Return the Security Pass

You walk up to the queuing people, holding up the green security pass. "Excuse me, does anyone know Ortopa Baskirl?"

Most of them ignore you, except an olive-skinned man with no eyebrows, who grabs the security pass. "Where'd you nick this from?"

What? "I didn't, I found it."

"Where's Ortopa?"

"How would I know?"

He turns to at the queue of people. "Anyone seen Ortopa today?"

While he's distracted, you run, ignoring his yelling and swearing, hoping he doesn't chase after you. Luckily, he doesn't. He probably doesn't want to be late for work – workers at the front of the queue have started climbing the ladder up to the over-city.

Okay, that's far too much excitement for one day – time to head back to Deadline Delivery for your next delivery job.

A few blocks from the Tollgate, you realize someone's following you. Two someones, in fact. Big guys. Maybe pirates, maybe muggers.

You stop, take off your backpack, turn it upside down and shake it to show there's nothing inside, hoping they'll give up once they know you're not carrying anything worth stealing.

Doesn't work – they're still following you.

At the next corner, you clatter over a bridge of floating oil drums and run for a nearby alley.

They follow. As you emerge on the street at the other end of the alley, you can see the Tollgate in the distance. Safety. Except that between you and the Tollgate is a speedboat, which roars into life when the crew see you. Muggers, slavers, or cannibals, whoever they are – you're surrounded.

Your only hope is to cross the road, and get to that brick building on the other side of the water. It has a narrow hole in its side wall, too tight for most adults to get through – a great escape route. If you can get to it.

Unfortunately, there are no bridges on this block, and you can't swim, even your dog-paddling is terrible. The speedboat will be here in a minute, tops.

Just as you think things can't get worse, there's barking and growling behind you. It's those wild dogs again, only a few yards away, and leading them is the huge German Shepherd with a ripped left ear. The two guys in the alley see the dogs, stop and keep their distance.

And that's when you remember the wrapped slice of meatloaf in your pocket, left over from breakfast. You toss it to the German Shepherd, which gobbles it down then licks your face while you scratch behind its ears.

"Help me?" you beg. "Over the road? Please?"

It's a smart dog – it's already spotted the speedboat, and the men in the alley. But is it smart enough to understand you? And does it want to help you?

"Help!" you yell, leap into the water, and dog-paddle for

your life. You swallow water and choke, expecting to drown. But suddenly there's wet fur under your hands, and the big dog is towing you through the water to the other side of the street.

"Thank you," you say, as you squeeze through the hole in the brick wall, with seconds to spare.

The dogs and the people on the boat growl at each other for a few seconds, then the boat roars away.

"Thank you," you repeat, reaching back through the hole and patting the German Shepherd. "Double, no, triple meatloaf for you tomorrow."

Congratulations, this part of your story is over. You're wet and tired and late getting back to Deadline delivery, but you've survived a dangerous day. What might have happened up in the over-city? Or if you'd done things differently around the Kannibal Krew and the Piranhas?

It's time to make a decision. Do you:

Go to the list of choices and start reading from another part of the story? **P122**

Or

Go back to the beginning and try another path? **P1**

Hope the Pirates Fight Each Other

The two Kannibal Krew reach the top of the stairs and run past the pillar you're hiding behind. Then they see the Piranhas, and stop so quickly that one crashes into the other. The Piranhas turn, equally surprised.

While both groups of pirates yell at each other, you sneak back down the way you came, unnoticed.

Brilliant.

But you soon hear running and raised voices behind you. Oh, of course, the outnumbered Kannibals are trying to escape down the same stairs you're on, and the Piranhas are chasing them.

Not so brilliant.

You leap down the stairs, two at a time, and slip, landing heavily at the bottom. Limping, you stagger past the Kannibals' red speedboat and hide behind an ancient fridge half-covered in broken bricks. Not much of a hiding place, but hopefully the pirates are more interested in each other than you. In the distance, the old woman's cabbage boat chugs away as fast as it can.

Seconds later, the two Kannibals dash out and leap onto their speedboat. The skull-faced man pushes the boat out into the water with a pole, while the Mohawked woman starts the engine. Or tries to – there's a whirring noise but nothing more. The man tries to start the engine too, but still nothing. They loudly blame each other. Hmm, you can see something they can't – wet handprints on the boat's stern, as if someone's been there in the last few minutes. Maybe they did something to the engine? But who?

Piranhas run out onto the sidewalk and screech to a halt – the boat is now several yards away from the sidewalk edge, probably too far to jump. One Piranha tries anyway, but instead lands in the muddy water with a huge splash. He coughs and curses, then dogpaddles through the floating trash towards the boat.

Abruptly, he vanishes under the surface. Didn't look like a dive, more like he was pulled down. By what? Froggies? The pirates stare at the water, as mystified as you are. Then they start yelling threats and throwing things at each other again.

Fine. So long as they're not yelling and throwing things at you.

Your left foot hurts, but you limp away.

Ahead is a rickety wooden sidewalk, its planks partially covered with flattened cardboard cartons. Or so you think, until you step straight through cardboard into thin air, and fall into the dirty water below. Weighed down by your backpack, shoes and clothes, you slowly sink.

An octopus swims through the murk and pulls off your backpack. No, impossible. Must be a hallucination – you remember reading somewhere that people see all sorts of impossible things when they're close to dying. The octopus somehow grows two brown arms and a body with green webbed feet. No, it's an octopus eating someone head first. No, that doesn't make sense either.

The creature drags you away, then pushes you up to the

surface. You gasp for breath, coughing and spluttering and holding onto what feels like a rotting plank. Thick mud squishes between your knees, and there's nothing under your feet. The only light comes from one side. Where is this?

You cough again, and retch.

"Shut up," says the octopus. Oh, it's a girl, wearing a rubbery octopus mask over her head. She must be a froggy, yeah, that would explain the webbed feet too. Drowning would have been preferable, if half the stories about froggies are true. Worse than cannibals, people say.

She holds your plastic-wrapped package. With her other hand, she points a rusty harpoon at you. "Hate you." She points towards the light. "Hate them more."

You peer out, and realize you're under a sidewalk – the same sidewalk you were standing on before. On the other side of the street, the pirates are still shouting, but no longer at each other.

Grappling hooks and ropes have capsized the red speedboat. The Mohawked woman is shrieking and splashing somewhere in the water. There's no sign of the skull-faced man. Two Piranhas have ropes lassoed around their bodies and are being slowly pulled into the water, despite the other Piranhas trying to pull them back or cut the ropes. Some Piranhas are throwing bricks and rubble into the water, as if desperately hoping to hit someone or something.

As you watch, a nearby patch of floating trash rises a few

inches above the surface and makes a kerchink noise. Something shoots out and hits a Piranha, who screams and falls to the sidewalk, next to the unmoving body of another pirate.

You hate pirates too, but not as much as these froggies do.

Out of the water next to you rises another pile of trash, with a man's mustachioed face underneath. (Unless it's a woman with a moustache – you're not going to ask.) He and the octopus girl peer at your delivery package and argue in loud whispers, glancing at you now and then. "Dry skins not for fungus deciding," he insists. "Verdigris afterwards delivery. Now fungus."

Or something like that – apparently froggies talk a special froggy language, and in a special froggy accent.

The mustachioed man disappears back under the water.

The octopus girl sighs, mutters to herself, and turns towards you. She's still holding that harpoon – and your package.

"That's not yours," you protest.

"Not yours either," she snarls, and shoves it back at you. Then she swims away, dragging you along by your shirt collar.

"I can't swim," you splutter, flopping around on your back, trying to breathe, trying to hold on to the package.

"True that." She takes you mostly under the shadow of sidewalks and buildings, and sometimes under piles of floating trash to cross streets. And once through a dark tunnel that seems to go right under a building from one street to the next. You try to keep track of the passing streets but are soon completely lost – the whole city looks different from down here.

At last she stops, by a steel ladder. The water's only waist-deep here, so you stand up. Above is a thick metal grate, with "390" scrawled next to it in orange spray-paint. Through the grate you can see part of a fluorescent light tube and a white ceiling.

"Hello, Chopper," she calls up.

A huge grey dog – presumably Chopper – looks down through the grate, and barks until a woman comes over and looks down too. She's wearing a white coat, a bulletproof vest, and a puzzled look.

"Delivery, 390 Brine," says the octopus girl.

This is Brine Street? You hold up the package, hoping the plastic wrapping hasn't leaked.

The woman frowns, looking at your cap. "Miss Betty's hiring froggies now?"

"I'm not a froggy," you protest.

"True that," agrees the girl.

The woman shrugs, unlocks the grate and swings it open. The girl pushes you up the ladder.

At the top is the whitest, cleanest room you've ever seen. What's that half-flower half-chemical smell?

Chopper stares at you, growling softly. He has no back legs, just two wheels held on with a frame of rods and straps. Even so, you're pretty sure he could still eat you alive if he wanted to, so you stay on the ladder, ready to drop back down if necessary.

The woman takes the package, slits it open and pulls out some finger-sized bottles. What would anyone put in bottles that small?

Chopper sniffs your trousers. Oh, your leftover meatloaf from breakfast. You pull the sodden bag from your pocket. What a yucky mess. "It's all yours, Chopper."

He swallows the lot in seconds, licks the bag, then licks your face.

"Okay, that's fine, thanks." The woman shows you a tablet screen displaying the Deadline Delivery web site, and presses the green Delivery Received icon. "Bye."

Just as you're wondering whether to try to escape up here, the octopus girl grabs your ankle and motions you back down with her harpoon.

"Um, bye." As you clamber down the ladder, the grate's closed and locked above you. "What is that place?" you ask the girl.

"Medical clinic. Obvious. No more nice – I save you only for package. Clinic good to froggies."

Huh? She saved you from drowning only because the package was for this clinic? If the package is that important, why not kill you and deliver it herself?

"Now verdigris," she says, grabs you by your shirt collar again and swims away again.

Verdigris? The mustachioed man said something about that too. Isn't verdigris the bluey-greeny stain you see on old copper and brass? What on earth is she talking about? Stupid froggies.

Perhaps ten minutes later, you arrive at a huge gloomy room with white tiled walls, balconies of seats on both sides and strange tall ladders at one end…oh, it's an indoor swimming pool, like you've seen in photos from the olden days. Why people back then needed a special room just for swimming, you don't know.

No-one's been swimming here since the city flooded. The tiles are lined with grimy horizontal tide marks – this whole room must flood every high tide. The pool is half-full of muddy water, and its far end has a large jagged hole, with daylight streaming in through it. More murky light filters in through dirty frosted glass windows along the room's walls.

Hundreds of froggies crowd the balconies above. To your surprise, none of them have claws, or fangs, or green skin, or webbed feet, like in the stories – they're just ordinary people. Except for their clothes, which are made from recycled…stuff, everything from plastic bags to metal bits to electrical cables. Lots of them wear hats or masks covered in trash – as disguises, presumably – and some wear goggles and web-toed flippers, also made from trash.

They all talk weird, like the octopus girl. But by listening hard, you realize some important stuff. Queen Verdigris is the name of their boss, a tall pale woman sitting on a deckchair on a tiny platform at the top of the tallest ladder, wearing a brass helmet from an old-fashioned diving suit. Fungus is the name of the girl in the octopus mask. "Dry-skins" is what they call anyone who isn't a froggy – under-city people, pirates, over-city people, even you. Not that you're dry at the moment.

Most importantly, the froggies are arguing about you. About whether to kill you.

"Dry-skin has seen too much froggy secrets," says one, and lots of froggies nod.

"Dry-skin run from pirates, just like us, sympathy," another says, and lots of froggies nod at that too.

"Dry-skin deliver for Brine Street clinic," Fungus points out. Is she trying to help you?

After a while, Queen Verdigris bangs on her ladder. Everyone quietens down and looks up at her expectantly. "Crocodile Doom," she announces in a gravelly voice.

A few people grumble, including Fungus, but most of them nod and shout, "Crocodile Doom!"

They're going to feed you to crocodiles? Is this their idea of fun? Maybe they don't have television down here.

Fungus shakes her head and mutters to herself, then pushes you into the pool.

The water's less than waist-deep, and not too cold. Too muddy to see what's below. As you stand, something crunches under your left foot and something else wriggles under your right foot.

Now what? Froggies with long spears are watching you from the pool edges, so clearly there's no point in trying to climb out of the pool. Try to escape out the hole in the far end of the pool? Seems too easy. Maybe it's a trap, and a hundred hungry crocodiles are hiding under the water, waiting. Or maybe this is all some stupid froggy joke, and someone wearing a crocodile mask will jump out and yell "Boo!" and everyone will laugh. Probably not though.

"Doom!" chant the froggies. "Doom! Doom!" Over and over again.

Something moves under the water, creating a line of ripples heading in your direction.

The froggies see the ripples too, and cheer.

"Doom! Doom!" chant a line of little froggy kids at the front row of a balcony, stomping their feet.

You're scared, but staying here and waiting to die seems pointless. So you start wading across the pool, trying not to trip on the slimy debris under your feet, and trying not to splash too much. Doesn't work though – the ripples change direction to follow you. For just a moment, something long and scaly breaks the surface then submerges again.

Above, the shouting and stomping get louder and louder. Then something heavy screeches and snaps, someone screams, and the froggies start shouting and pointing. You look up and see a balcony's partly collapsed, probably from all that foot stomping. From a broken guard rail, a little froggy kid is dangling down over the pool.

It's time to make a decision, and fast. Do you:

Run for the hole in the far wall while everyone's distracted? **P119**

Or

Help the froggy kid? **P94**

Help the Froggy Kid

Trying to ignore the ripple from the approaching crocodile, you splash over to the broken balcony, and are just in time to catch the froggy kid as he screams and falls.

Ropes wrap around you both and you're dragged up into the air together. Just in time – moments later, a huge crocodile bursts out of the water, its long jaws snapping inches from your feet.

Hands pull you both up to a safer part of the balcony. Around you, dozens of voices yell and give advice and bicker all at the same time.

"Shut up!" Fungus shouts.

Everyone does. There's silence, except for the crocodile still snapping its jaws and thrashing around below, probably wondering where its lunch has gone, and the little froggy kid, crying in Fungus's arms.

"Why?" she demands, glaring at you. "Why help my bro Bucket?"

That's her little brother? What sort of name's Bucket? Although admittedly, it's no weirder than the name Fungus.

"I couldn't…do nothing and let a little kid get eaten alive," you say.

Bucket leans over and hugs you.

Queen Verdigris bangs on her ladder, and points at you. "Froggy friend," she announces.

Everyone cheers, and starts chanting, "Froggy friend," over and over. These froggies sure do like their chanting.

There's no more foot stomping though, and everyone's keeping away from the balcony edges.

What "froggy friend" means, you're not sure, but it must be something good, coz everyone's smiling and no one's trying to feed you to crocodiles any more.

"Lunch," Queen Verdigris announces.

Everyone cheers again. For a horrible moment, you think maybe she means that you'll *be* their lunch, but they take you to a nearby room full of long tables and wonderful foody smells, and the queen insists you sit next to her. Fungus and Bucket sit on your other side, and Bucket gives you lots of shy smiles.

The food is…weird, like everything else down here, but it tastes as good as it smells, even if you can't tell what some of it is.

"Good, yes?" Queen Verdigris asks.

"It's the best meal I've had in months, your majesty," you say, and she looks pleased.

You gradually get used to their odd accent and language. They're talking about ordinary things – fishing, growing vegetables, recycling, playing sport, keeping safe, finding clean water and food. Sounds like life is even tougher for froggies than people like you, because absolutely everyone picks on froggies – not just pirates, but most under-city people too. You feel guilty, remembering the horrible gossip you'd heard and believed about froggies – almost none of it was true.

To be honest, now that the froggies have stopped trying

to feed you to the crocodiles, they seem nicer than most under-city people you've known. They're like one huge family, all looking after each other. Not like most dry-skins.

"You froggy friend now," says Queen Verdigris. "We like you. So stay, be one of us, yes?"

Is she serious? "Become a froggy? Forever?" Part of their family?

She nods. Fungus and Bucket gaze at you, grinning.

It's time to make a decision. Do you:

Become a froggy? **P97**

Or

Stay a courier, and return to Deadline Delivery? **P111**

Become a Froggy

"Yes, I want to be a froggy." Your voice shakes a little. You won't be sorry to never see Deadline Delivery again (even though Miss Betty owes you ten dollars for the Brine Street clinic delivery), but giving up your old life is scary. What if this is a terrible mistake?

Froggies hug you and shake your hand.

"Fungus, find new froggy a job," Queen Verdigris orders.

Fungus nods. So does Bucket, even though no one asked him.

After lunch, they take you along dozens of gloomy tunnels and passageways, sometimes walking or wading, sometimes swimming and towing you. "Careful not get lost," Fungus says. "Tide rising now, some tunnels soon flood."

"I'm already lost, and I can't swim."

"We teach you," Bucket says, and Fungus nods.

Eventually they stop, in a huge hall that smells like a giant fart. There are tanks and pipes everywhere, and pulleys and pistons turning enormous wheels, and dozens of froggies busy on a long raised platform.

"Crabb Street sewage treatment plant," Fungus says proudly. "Filter sewer for city south suburbs."

"Mmm," you reply, trying to hold your breath.

"Stinky water down from over-city," Bucket explains, pointing to a row of pipes. "Clean water up to over-city." He points to another row of pipes.

They take you over to the long raised platform, where froggies are pushing giant sieves through a long tank of what Bucket calls "stinky water", and occasionally pulling out things like bottles and rags and rusty cans.

"Recycling," Fungus says. "Many things found, sometimes valuable – jewelry, phones, coins. We sell back to over-city."

You hope they wash the recycled stuff really, really well.

"And sell stinky sludge back to over-city for fertilizer," adds Bucket, who seems to be an expert on stinky stuff.

Perhaps they can see you're not too impressed by sewage. They take you up and down more tunnels and corridors and streets for what seems like an hour. The farty smell is replaced by a fishy smell, getting stronger.

In the distance, at the end of a wide tunnel, you see bright light and water. Lots of water. More water than you've ever seen before. And the fishiest smell you've ever smelled before.

You reach the end of the tunnel, stop on a large platform and gaze out at the sea. Obviously, this is exactly the same sea which flows through the city streets. But you've never seen it like this before, with no buildings or security fences in the way, just endless waves, all the way to the horizon, under the biggest, emptiest sky ever.

To one side of the platform is a long boat full of glittering fish. On board is a golden-skinned woman with tiger stripe tattoos on her face. She frowns up at you.

"Move," snarls a voice beside you. Four froggies push

trolleys with crates full of fish past you and down the tunnel. That looks like hard work.

Fungus turns to you and crosses her arms. Bucket copies her. "Which job? Sewage or fish?" she asks.

Not much of a choice. What about exciting jobs, like feeding the crocodiles, or ambushing pirates?

Anyway, it's time to make a decision. Do you:

Work at the sewage treatment plant? **P100**

Or

Work at the fishery? **P104**

Sewage Treatment

"Sewage," you say glumly. You're not looking forward to working in that stinky sewage treatment plant, but you feel unsafe here by the sea – there's just…too much water.

After a few days working at the sewage treatment plant, you hardly notice the smell any more. Or maybe your nose has stopped working.

Anyway, the work's okay. One day you find seven one-dollar coins in your sludge sieve – it's amazing what over-city people lose down drains.

There's more to the job than just sieving sludge. You also learn how to clean tanks and pipes, to oil pistons and scrape filters, and to shovel dried sludge (which luckily smells better than wet sludge) into sacks labeled "All-Natural Organic Fertilizer".

At night, whenever the tide is right, you join groups of froggies outside, walking through the watery streets on long stilts, to collect recyclable bottles, cans and plastic. At first, you feel silly disguising yourself in a trash suit and hiding in the water whenever dry-skins walk by, but you soon start enjoying being a sneaky froggy. And it's fun helping the others scare away any dry-skins who get too close to the maze of froggy tunnels.

Fungus and Bucket teach you to swim. You're still terrible at it, but less terrible than before, and getting better every day – or so they claim.

Fog, the sewage treatment plant manager, says you're

getting better at sieving sludge too.

Two weeks later, you spot something glinting in the sludge tank. Jewelry perhaps? Someone found a wedding ring down here last month. You grab at the glint with your sieve.

Wow. It's jewelry alright – a golden necklace, glittering with sparkly gemstones.

"Shiny," says everyone.

It sure is. But is it real gold and real gems?

Fog washes the necklace, examines it carefully, and then makes half a dozen phone calls. "Real," he tells you. "Worth fortune. Over-city owner offering return reward. Huge reward. Take now to Queen Verdigris."

You do.

"So pretty," the queen says with a sigh, holding the necklace up to the light. "Shame we can't keep."

"Yes, your majesty." You know the froggies never keep found valuables – that would be stealing, and would make froggies no better than pirates. But there's nothing wrong with claiming a reward. Even a huge reward.

"What to do with shiny reward? What you think?"

"Me, your majesty?"

"Yes, you find, so what you think, what to do? Maybe I agree, maybe not, but tell me even so."

"Well, um, I've only been a froggy for a few weeks, but, um, I was wondering…"

"Yes, yes?"

"Why don't we start a froggy courier business? We know

a million routes around the city that dry-skins don't, and I reckon we could deliver stuff faster than anyone else. We'd make money, and…well, people might start treating froggies better if they knew we weren't monsters, just ordinary people making an honest living."

"Hmm," she says. "Hmm, hmm, hmm."

That afternoon, there's a meeting in the swimming pool room, and everyone else says "hmm" and argues and complains and disagrees.

After an hour or so, they mostly agree that a froggy courier business is a good idea.

There's only one problem – other than you, no one's brave enough to be a courier.

But then Fungus stands up. "I be courier too." She turns to you. "If you teach me."

"And me," Bucket insists, sticking his bottom lip out.

He's far too young, you almost say. But then again, he's a far better swimmer than you, and can run faster than a hungry rat, so why not?

"Sure," you say. "Let's do it."

Congratulations, this part of your story is over. You've survived pirates and crocodiles and found a new life for yourself.

And now, starting a courier business could change the lives of your new froggy family.

Things could have turned out very differently if you'd made different decisions. Maybe better, maybe worse.

It's time to make a decision. Do you:

Go to the list of choices and start reading from another part of the story? **P122**

Or

Go back to the beginning and try another path? **P1**

Fish

"Fish," you say glumly. All those fish smell really…fishy, but working here sounds (and smells) better than stinky sewage.

"New worker for you, Tiger Lily," Fungus tells the woman with tiger-stripe tattoos, then she and Bucket just walk off and leave you there.

From the fishing boat, Tiger Lily frowns at you again. "Can you swim, kid?" She has a strange accent.

"Not really, ma'am. Not yet."

"Call me captain, not ma'am. Can you catch fish?"

"No, captain. Well, I once found a small fish in my shirt after falling into the water – does that count?"

She rolls her eyes. "Can you push a trolley?"

"Not far, if it's full of crates of fish."

"Ever been to sea?"

"This is the first time I've even seen the open sea."

Some of the fishing boat's crew snigger.

Captain Tiger Lily rolls her eyes and gives a loud sigh. "Alright, get down here and help unload these fish."

"Captain, why don't you talk funny like the other froggies?"

More sniggering from the crew.

The captain glares at you. "What a nosy child. This is how everyone talked back in the over-city, where I was born."

"You left the over-city to become a froggy? Why?"

"Less talking and lift that fish crate, kid."

"Yes, captain."

After the crates have been unloaded and sent down the tunnel on trolleys, the crew do mysterious things with ropes and nets and sails, while you try to stay out of their way. Then the boat starts swaying and rocking and you realize it's moving, heading out to sea. Looking back, the city gets smaller and smaller. Will you ever see it again?

A wrinkled crewman claps you on the shoulder. "Feeling seasick yet, kid?" he asks cheerfully. "I still remember my first boat trip – I spent the whole time leaning over the railing, throwing up and groaning and wanting to die." He looks around at the other crew with a grin. "Two dollars says the kid will throw up in the next ten minutes!"

The crew laugh, and make complicated bets on how soon you'll throw up and how often.

The captain doesn't join in the laughter or the gambling, but she is watching you carefully.

This must be a test – if you fail, she'll probably send you to the sewage treatment plant. So you clutch a handrail, trying to ignore your lurching stomach, and wishing you hadn't eaten so much lunch. Closing your eyes doesn't help, and looking at the boat's deck makes it worse. Staring at the horizon helps you feel a little better.

Perhaps half an hour later, the sails are lowered, and the boat slows and stops in the middle of empty sea. To everyone's surprise, especially yours, you haven't thrown up even once.

"Well done, kid," says the wrinkled crewman, grinning even though he's lost his bet. "Perhaps we'll make a sailor out of you after all."

Lots of money changes hands. No one seems annoyed at you.

You spot fins approaching the boat. "Sharks!" you shout.

Everyone roars with laughter.

Even the captain smiles. "They're dolphins, our fishing partners."

Several dolphins stick their heads out of the water and they laugh at you too – well, not really, but that's what it looks and sounds like.

The captain whistles at the dolphins. They click and whistle back – they're talking! – then race away.

She shouts orders to the crew.

In the distance, the dolphins are returning.

"Wait," orders the captain, watching them through binoculars. "Wait…wait…ready…now!"

The crew launch a huge spring-powered net over the waves. It falls just in front of the dolphins, and the water fills with furious splashing from fish caught in the net.

As the captain shouts orders, everyone hauls the net in, even you. Dozens of ropes have to be pulled and tightened in just the right order. At just the wrong moment, you pull on the wrong rope and hundreds of fish spill from the net. The dolphins snap them up.

The captain bares her teeth and growls at you, looking more like a tiger than ever.

"Sorry," you mumble.

"The dolphins deserve their share," she snaps. "But not

quite that much."

Desperate not to make any more mistakes, you watch and listen carefully, and do whatever anyone tells you. It's especially hard because the bits of the boat have such weird names, like the halyard – the line that raises and lowers the sail. And the boom – the horizontal pole at the bottom of the sail, that's nearly knocked you on the head twice already.

On the voyage back to the city, you don't make any more embarrassing mistakes or throw up. Sailing's cooler than you'd expected.

But during unloading back at the dock, you drop and nearly spill a crate of fish.

Captain Tiger Lily glares at you again. "See you tomorrow, 6AM," is all she says.

Tomorrow? So she wants you back, and you won't be sent to the sewage treatment plant? Yay!

Weeks go by. You go out fishing most days. Soon you can name all the boat's weird bits, know how to tie half a dozen different knots, can tack and jibe and trim as well as any of the crew, and duck under a swinging boom without even thinking about it. Sailing's hard work, even harder than being a courier, but the best fun ever.

Except for fish. Not the smell, you're used to that. But they're so slimy and slippery and wiggly and…fishy. You're always dropping them, or stepping on them, or tangling the fishing net, or doing something wrong. Every time, the captain rolls her eyes. Or sighs. Or both.

Most evenings, you're exhausted, but go for swimming

lessons with Fungus and Bucket whenever they offer – a real sailor needs to be able to swim.

One morning at the dock, you see the captain talking with Queen Verdigris. They see you watching them, and turn away. If the queen's involved, this must be something serious. What if she decides you can't be a sailor anymore? Or worse, what if you can't even be a froggy?

They're walking over to you. Uh-oh.

"Would you like to hear a secret?" Tiger Lily asks you. "I hate fish. I hate catching them, hate their smell, don't even like eating them. Well, except for Swab's fish curry, but Swab can make anything taste good. So then why, you may ask, did I leave the over-city to come down here and captain a smelly old fishing boat?"

Good question, but you stay quiet, hoping she'll say more.

"Because I love sailboats," she continues. "I've loved them since I was a small child, staring out to the sea from the window in our thirty-ninth floor apartment." She points up to the over-city towers. "I gave up everything to sail. But even so, I wish there was more to froggy sailing than fishing. Don't you?"

You nod. "Sailing's like flying on the water."

She grins. "Yeah, you get it too. I could see that on your first day. Ever heard of Oasis?"

"The magical island where there's no over-city and no pirates, and froggies can live in peace and safety? That's Bucket's favorite bedtime story."

Queen Verdigris gives a mysterious smile. "More than

bedtime story."

"What? Oasis is real?"

"Maybe," Tiger Lily says. "I've collected all the Oasis stories I've ever heard, and half of them contradict each other. But still, I reckon Oasis is worth looking for. And if it doesn't exist, perhaps we'll find another island to turn into Oasis. So, I'm looking for brave sailors to join my crew."

"Me?"

Queen Verdigris laughs. "Yes, you. Why else we talking, huh?"

"It'll be dangerous," Tiger Lily warns you. "We may never return."

"Living here's dangerous too. I'm in."

It's not quite that simple. Queen Verdigris has bought Tiger Lily a boat – the Seahorse, named after an olden-days animal that could run underwater, or so Fungus say – but the Seahorse is old and leaks and needs lots of repairs. There are a dozen more crew to choose, and food and water and tools and weapons and a million other things to organize for the voyage.

But somehow everything gets done. A month later, you and Tiger Lily and the rest of the crew board the Seahorse, watched by nearly every froggy in the city. Bucket's crying because he wanted to come on the voyage too. You wave goodbye to everyone, knowing you'll miss them, wondering if you'll ever see them again. Or the city.

"Cast off. Make sail," orders Tiger Lily.

"Aye, captain." Blinking back tears, you turn to face the

oncoming sea, and adventure.

Congratulations, this part of your story is over – who knows what the future will hold? And what might have happened if you'd made different decisions? Could you have ended up in the over-city? Or in the clutches of pirates?

It's time to make a decision. Do you:

Go to the list of choices and start reading from another part of the story? **P122**

Or

Go back to the beginning and try another path? **P1**

Return to Deadline Delivery

"Thanks, but I have to get back to my job," you tell Queen Verdigris. Not that it's much of a job. "But…I'd really like to visit again some time. If you'll let me."

She smiles. "You froggy friend forever."

After lunch, Fungus and Bucket tow you back to Nori Road near Ivory Tower, using a special secret froggy route that goes right under Big Pig's Wall – no toll fee to pay, yay!

Bucket's only half your age, but he can swim like…um, a frog.

"I wish I could swim," you tell him. Working as a courier would be so much easier if you could use secret froggy routes.

"We teach you," Bucket says, and Fungus nods.

You all say goodbye. A few minutes later, you're back at Deadline Delivery.

Miss Betty scowls at you. "You're late."

Late? "I was attacked by Kannibal Krew, Piranhas, and a crocodile!" And by froggies too, sort of…but not really. You're not going to say anything bad about the froggies.

"No excuses!" She counts out eight one-dollar coins.

"Eight? You said the job paid ten dollars."

She gives a sour grin and points to your dripping cap. "Minus two dollars – Wet Uniform fee."

So unfair. Maybe you should've become a froggy. Bet no one makes them wear stupid caps or pay stupid fees.

Miss Betty drops a long blue box on the counter. "Urgent

delivery, Crabb Street. Pays nine bucks."

You sigh, nod, and take the box.

The steel door squeaks and starts to close, and you hurry out. Miss Betty doesn't say goodbye. She never does.

Congratulations, this part of your story is over. You have learned the truth about the froggies, and made new friends. Things could have happened very differently – you might have ended up in the over-city, or as a pirate slave, or rich, or broke, or with a different job. Or eaten by crocodiles.

It's time to make a decision. Do you:

Go to the list of choices and start reading from another part of the story? **P122**

Or

Go back to the beginning and try another path? **P1**

Become the Clinic Courier

Doctor Hurst was right – working as courier for the Brine Street Community Medical Clinic has been really hard work, and some days it's just as dangerous as your old job. But every day, you're thankful there's no more Deadline Delivery and no more Miss Betty. Never again.

The clinic feeds you, and pays you – pays you well. And they give you free treatment for gun wounds, rat bites, and plague mold.

On the downside, they also make you shower every single week, whether you need it or not.

You don't mind…too much.

Congratulations, this part of your story is over. You have a brand new life, and who knows where it might lead. What might have happened if you'd never taken that ride on the cabbage boat? Or not gone through the secret tunnel at all?

It's time to make a decision. Do you:

Go to the list of choices and start reading from another part of the story? **P122**

Or

Go back to the beginning and try another path? **P1**

Run from the Kannibals

You twist out of the old man's grasp and sprint past the slowing speedboat.

You'll be a goner as soon as that speedboat has time to change direction and follow you, but maybe you can get out of sight before that happens, and before the old man can chase you down.

Diving through the next doorway, you race down a short alley, then up a tall fire escape ladder.

Bad mistake. Every footstep clangs on the steel. Now he'll know exactly where you are.

Sure enough, you soon hear him at the bottom of the ladder, grunting and swearing.

At the top of the ladder is a mossy brick wall with a small window, its glass long gone.

No other exit, except a thirty-foot drop onto concrete. You're trapped. Unless you can squeeze through the window? Yeah, the pirates are bigger than you and won't be able to follow. Unless they send that scary baby in after you, ha ha.

You push your backpack through the window, then follow it. Your head and shoulders get through ok, just, but then your hips get stuck. The old man's footsteps on the ladder are getting louder – he must be close to the top. No way do you want to die halfway through a window, pirates eating you from the toes up.

Desperately, you wiggle your hips. Something rips and

you're through. Back on your feet, you grab the backpack and run, run, run, ignoring the old man yelling that you're a "crazy kid".

You keep running, sometimes aiming for Tollgate and safety, but mostly at random, until your lungs shudder and legs shake and you fall to the floor of a moldy-walled walkway.

Lying there, gasping, you suddenly realize what ripped earlier – your trouser pocket with all your money. It's all gone. Every last coin.

How will you get through Tollgate now?

Once you get your breath back, you work out where you are – four blocks from Tollgate – and carefully make your way there, because maybe you're still being followed. But the sidewalks are more crowded with people around here, and there's safety in numbers – or at least a better chance of someone raising the alarm if pirates are spotted.

And then you wait.

Hoping you'll see someone you know, someone who'll loan you a dollar.

You don't.

Hoping someone will feel sorry for your sad face, ripped clothes and bandaged shotgun wounds.

Fat chance.

Hoping a soft-hearted Gate guard is on duty.

No such thing.

The sun sets, and you're still stuck outside the Wall. Everyone's heard the stories about things which come out to hunt the streets at night. Things even worse than pirates and froggies. Just stories to frighten little kids, you tell yourself.

In what's left of the twilight, you find a hidey-hole between a collapsed wall and a sheet of rusty corrugated iron. Your dinner is the last crumbs from the meatloaf plastic bag in your pocket. You hug your knees to stay warm, and try to sleep, hoping something nasty won't find you in the middle of the night, hoping that tomorrow will be better.

This part of your story is over. Today was a disaster, but at least you're still alive. Would things have gone better if you'd taken that clinic courier job? Or stayed away from that old woman and her cabbage boat?

It's time to make a decision. Do you:

Go to the list of choices and start reading from another part of the story? **P122**

Or

Go back to the beginning and try another path? **P1**

Follow the Old Man's Orders

The Mohawk woman laughs at you, and the baby joins in. The bald man with the huge skull tattoo twists his mouth into either a smile or a snarl, it's hard to tell.

"What's so funny?" growls the old man.

"Your face," the woman tells him.

"Baa!" says the baby.

"Crazy kid," the old man tells you.

"What?" you say, completely confused. And surprised to still be alive.

"We know you're a courier, cap or no cap," he continues. "We saw you back at the clinic."

This is a robbery? They want Doctor Hurst's package, whatever it is?

"We do what we can to help the clinic, so we got you a present," the woman says. She tosses something to you.

You flinch, expecting something horrible.

The old man grabs it from mid-air and waves it in front of you. It's a necklace – alternating yellow and black plastic bottle tops and half a dozen human teeth on a long black string. Horrible, but not quite as horrible as you'd expected.

He places the necklace around your neck. "Any time you're in Kannibal Krew territory, just show this and no Kannibal will bother you."

"Um," you say, still confused.

The skull tattoo man frowns at you. "Well? Say thank you!"

"Thank you," you say. "I mean it. Thank you. Really."

The old man grunts. "You're welcome." He hops down into the boat and it roars off before you can say another word.

You hide the necklace under your shirt, put your Deadline Delivery cap back on, and walk the six blocks back to Tollgate, thinking hard. Safe passage through Kannibal Krew territory, forever? A necklace like this is worth its weight in gold, to any courier. After paying your toll, you jog to Nori Road and deliver Doctor Hurst's package to 157, then return to Ivory Tower and Deadline Delivery.

Miss Betty scowls at you. As usual. But pays you the ten-dollar delivery fee, as promised. That's thirty-two dollars in your pocket – you're rich! Well, a lot richer than usual.

The steel door squeaks and starts to close, and you hurry out. Miss Betty doesn't say goodbye. She never does.

This part of your story is over. Today turned out pretty well, and who knows where tomorrow might lead. But things could have turned out differently – you might have ended up in the clutches of much nastier pirates, or gone to the over-city, or been captured by froggies, or eaten by crocodiles.

It's time to make a decision. Do you:

Go to the list of choices and start reading from another part of the story? **P122**

Or

Go back to the beginning and try another path? **P1**

Run for the Hole

You wade as fast as you can to the other end of the pool.

The mysterious ripple doesn't follow you. As far as you can tell. It's hard to be sure, what with the other ripples from you, and from bits falling from the balcony.

The froggies rescue the dangling kid before it can fall in the water. Good on them. But then they remember you, and all the "Doom" chanting starts up again, sounding even angrier than before. Someone throws something at you, and it lands in the water just a couple of yards away.

You run out through the jagged hole.

But it's not an exit after all, just a smallish room with one wall of glass bricks.

Two doorways.

One's blocked by a fallen concrete beam.

The other's on the far side of a raised platform occupied by a family of crocodiles. They stare at you. Two of them hiss then slip into the water.

You turn and look out the hole, only to see that ripple again, heading straight for you. At the front of the ripple, a crocodilian snout and eyes appear. The last thing you ever see is its jaw opening wide.

I'm sorry, this part of your story is over. You escaped pirates and the crazy old cabbage boat woman, but you were foolish to think you could escape the froggies and their Crocodile Doom.

It's time to make a decision. Do you:

Go to the list of choices and start reading from another part of the story? **P122**

Or

Go back to the beginning and try another path? **P1**

List of Choices

More You Say Which Way Adventures.

YouSayWhichWay.com

More About the Author

Peter Friend is a New Zealand writer who's sold fiction, plays and articles to numerous magazines and anthologies around the world. This is his first interactive adventure book.

Printed in Great Britain
by Amazon

71163372R00078